SPECIAL MESSAGE TO READERS

THE ULVERSCROFT FOUNDATION
(registered UK charity number 264873)
was established in 1972 to provide funds for
research, diagnosis and treatment of eye diseases.
Examples of major projects funded by
the Ulverscroft Foundation are:-

- The Children's Eye Unit at Moorfields Eye Hospital, London
- The Ulverscroft Children's Eye Unit at Great Ormond Street Hospital for Sick Children
- Funding research into eye diseases and treatment at the Department of Ophthalmology, University of Leicester
- The Ulverscroft Vision Research Group, Institute of Child Health
- Twin operating theatres at the Western Ophthalmic Hospital, London
- The Chair of Ophthalmology at the Royal Australian College of Ophthalmologists

You can help further the work of the Foundation
by making a donation or leaving a legacy.
Every contribution is gratefully received. If you
would like to help support the Foundation or
require further information, please contact:

THE ULVERSCROFT FOUNDATION
The Green, Bradgate Road, Anstey
Leicester LE7 7FU, England
Tel: (0116) 236 4325

website: www.foundation.ulverscroft.com

A VERY SPECIAL GIRL

Though warned by her parents, Emma marries Nicholas Stagger, a Krasnovian from Traj. Too late she has found that her parents were right, for Nicky's infidelities are more than she can stand. Furthermore, Nicky's involvement in the politics of his own country brings Emma herself into danger; but it is through this involvement that she meets Paul, President of Krasnovia. At last Emma can see her future clearly, but danger still awaits . . .

RENÉE SHANN

◆

A VERY
SPECIAL
GIRL

Complete and Unabridged

LINFORD
Leicester

First published in Great Britain in 1975 by
Robert Hale & Company
London

First Linford Edition
published 2014
by arrangement with
Robert Hale Limited
London

A catalogue record for this book is available
from the British Library.

ISBN 978–1–4448–1902–1

Published by
F. A. Thorpe (Publishing)
Anstey, Leicestershire

Set by Words & Graphics Ltd.
Anstey, Leicestershire
Printed and bound in Great Britain by
T. J. International Ltd., Padstow, Cornwall

This book is printed on acid-free paper

1

Trafalgar Square was already crowded on that Saturday afternoon by the time Emma Lawson got there. She was jostled this way and that and she wished her friend Lucy Brent could have come with her. They had decided to attend the anti-vivisection meeting together as soon as they had seen it advertised. Lucy and she were dead against animals being subjected to the various tests that vivisection involved, even if they did further the cause of drugs and medicine.

But that Saturday morning Lucy had gone down with 'flu.

'I'll go on my own,' Emma told her mother after Lucy's mother had telephoned to say Lucy was in bed with a high temperature and the doctor had been sent for.

Mrs Lawson had tried to dissuade Emma.

'I don't like the idea of your going to a meeting by yourself,' she had said. 'In fact, as you know, I wasn't at all keen on your going even with Lucy, neither was your father, but you were both so set on it . . . '

Emma had kissed her mother goodbye and reminded her that she was eighteen and not eight, and assured her that she had nothing to worry about. All the same, she began to feel uneasy as the crowd jostled and harried her. It wasn't at all the kind of gathering she had visualized. She had expected to find a small group of well-behaved young people and tweedy wives from the Home Counties, listening earnestly to a speaker on the plinth describing the horrors of the laboratories. Instead, she found herself in the midst of an angry mob that filled the Square to overflowing and was exchanging insults with a political orator ranting into a microphone which shrieked and crackled through loudspeakers turned like guns on the crowd.

She had been there only a short time, being crushed by the noisy throng the nature of which she couldn't grasp, when a large, red-faced policeman with a fatherly manner appeared before her.

'Now what's a nice young lady like you doing with this scruffy lot?' he asked. 'Look out for your bag, Miss, or some bright lad'll nick it off you. If I were you I'd go along home.' Then to the people closing in on Emma: 'Come on now, move along.' And more imperatively : 'Move along, I said, or are the lot of you deaf?'

Emma edged out of the Square towards the pavement beneath the National Gallery, where there was more breathing space.

A gleaming-eyed young man with long, untidy dark hair who stood right beside her said fervently, 'We must stand shoulder to shoulder against the menace.'

'Maybe you're right,' she said doubtfully, not having a clue as to what he was talking about, but feeling she ought to agree with him.

'You feel as I do, don't you?' he demanded.

'I don't really know. Because, to be frank, I don't know what this meeting is about.'

'Holy smoke!' He gazed down at her out of dark piercing eyes. 'Come and have a cup of coffee with me and I'll tell you.'

She felt herself being swept along by him, not by any physical propulsion but by the magnetism of his personality.

'I'm Nicholas Stagger, known to my friends as Nicky,' he said as they sat down at a table for two at the Corner House.

She felt sure he imagined she would know who he was, but she couldn't remember ever having heard his name before.

'You are one of us, aren't you?' he asked. 'You must be or you wouldn't be at this demo.'

She hadn't a notion who 'us' might be. But the penny was beginning to

4

drop. This must be a students' rally, though what they were demonstrating against she had no idea. But she had never before seen gathered together so many long-haired, bearded, untidy young men or so many sloppy-jeaned, lanky-haired girls.

'To be honest, as I've just said, I don't know what this meeting is about. I have obviously turned up on the wrong day. I thought it was an anti-vivisection protest meeting.'

'An anti-vivisection meeting! I can't believe it. How wrong can you be?' ejaculated Nicholas Stagger.

'Is it a political demonstration?' Emma asked tentatively.

'Of course it is. What else is there in life except politics and love?'

Emma felt abysmally inadequate. She knew very little about politics and not much about love. She had had boyfriends, one or two of whom she had believed herself to be in love with, but she was certain that this young man was never likely to be one of them.

5

All the same, she couldn't deny that he attracted her even after such a brief acquaintance. She had never met anyone like him before.

'Politics and love are all that matter,' he said.

'I'm not so sure,' Emma said. 'After all, there is music and art and quite a lot else besides.'

Nicholas Stagger shrugged off music and art, remarking that they were only pastimes.

'Love and politics alone are real,' he repeated.

'I'm afraid I made a stupid mistake,' said Emma. 'As I've just told you, I didn't know it was a political meeting in Trafalgar Square today.'

She wanted to divert him from love and politics. Especially from love.

'The anti-vivisection meeting is next Saturday,' he said. 'Do you mean to tell me you have never heard of me? That is very strange. I come from Krasnovia.'

Emma could only suppose that Krasnovia had been one of those countries that had been called something else when she was at school. It hadn't been in the news for a long time. She thought of it vaguely as being near Greece, Yugoslavia or somewhere in that southern part of Europe.

'Eighteen months ago,' said Nicholas Stagger, 'there was a rising against the government. Tragically, there was a successful *coup d'état*. The legal government was overthrown. This was in all your newspapers. Surely you must have read of the fighting at the barricades in Traj?'

Emma remembered it dimly. But every day the newspapers and TV reported fighting and uprisings somewhere. It was difficult to keep track of them all.

'I think I do remember it now,' she said.

'Then you must have read about Nicholas Stagger who led the students to lift the siege of the post office in Traj.'

Emma felt breathless with excitement. This was certainly an unexpected turn in the events of the afternoon. Very different from what she had expected.

'When the rebels won,' he said, 'I escaped across the frontier in disguise. I came to London and claimed political asylum. It was granted to me. Now I live here. I became a naturalized Englishman and earn my bread and butter in the foreign department of the B.B.C., translating the Krasnovian newspapers and broadcasts into English.'

'That must be very interesting.'

'It isn't. It is dull. Destroying to a man of action.'

They gorged cream cakes and drank endless cups of coffee. Emma never had to bother about her figure, she was slender as a reed, whereas her friend Lucy was always watching her diet, terrified of putting on weight.

'What's your name?' Nicky asked.

'Emma Lawson.'

'Emma — isn't that a bit old-fashioned?'

'Not any more.'

'And you live — ?'

'In a village you will probably never have heard of. Hoxley Green, in Sussex. My father's the vicar there.'

Nicky put his head on one side and looked at her with a mixture of disbelief and increased interest.

'Can't say I'd have taken you for a vicar's daughter.'

'Looks are deceptive.'

'Have you a job?'

'Yes, in a little boutique in our nearest town.'

Having found out this much about Emma, Nicky took charge of the conversation. Emma scarcely spoke. Nicky talked all the time, mining deeper and deeper into his richest hoard, himself, throwing up great heaps of gold and dross for her enlightenment. She had never known any young man so frank. Especially as she was a total stranger. Nothing apparently embarrassed him. He was as outspoken about his discreditable escapades as his honourable triumphs, obviously convinced that everything relating to Nicholas Stagger must be of absorbing interest and worthy of respect. She felt almost as if she had become a little minnow trapped and floating in the bowl of his large liquid black eyes.

'Now,' he said when they had finished their coffee and cakes, 'we will go to my room.'

She stared at him. 'You must be joking.'

He looked at her as if he couldn't have heard her aright. 'I most certainly am not. Why not?'

'Because — because — ' Emma felt herself colouring. 'I don't know you. And even if I did — '

'You don't visit young men in their rooms unchaperoned?'

'No, I don't,' said Emma flatly. 'And anyway, I must go home.'

'You came to attend a meeting and, as you were in the Square for such a short time, there can't be all that hurry. I live only a short distance from here

— in Ebury Street. It will be a nice walk in the park under the trees most of the way or we'll take a taxi if you like.'

She shook her head. 'I don't think so.' But to her astonishment she felt a faint regret. What was there about Nicholas Stagger that made her, her heart beating faster, even consider that she would like to fall in with his suggestion?

'Are you a virgin?' he asked her.

'Really!' Her cheeks now were crimson and her hands were trembling.

'There is much in the English idiom that I find puzzling,' Nicky said. 'I put a simple question to you and you say 'really'. What does it mean? Either you are a virgin or you are not a virgin. It is not possible to be not really a virgin.'

'Of course I'm a virgin!' she said indignantly.

'How sad for you,' he said. 'So much good life wasted. Love is for every age, but it is at its best when we are young.'

'Please let's stop talking about it.'

'Oh, but I must talk to you about it,'

Nicky said earnestly. 'It is most important that you should know.'

'Possibly. But a conversation like this embarrasses me.'

'Why? Is it not true, real, simple? Why should such things be embarrassing?'

'I'm sure you think I'm very silly, but to me they are.'

'A woman's whole life can be ruined,' Nicky said, 'if her first lover is clumsy, unkind, inconsiderate. But I am very experienced and very kind.'

'I'm sure you're very experienced after all you've told me,' said Emma tartly.

'Then come to my room. I will not seduce you against your will. I do not like that. The whole success of a love affair is in its mutuality. I am a very moral person.'

Emma decided he was the most extraordinary young man she had ever met. She wondered what Lucy would have made of him. But if Lucy had been there she, Emma, wouldn't be

12

having a tête-à-tête with Nicholas Stagger. He might pick up one girl, but she doubted if he would have picked up two. Not with what he obviously had in mind.

She told herself she should get up, say a curt goodbye and leave him. She wasn't accustomed to strange men asking her to go back to their rooms with them. But somehow it wasn't easy to be offended. He was so disarming. Quite clearly he didn't consider his suggestion had been one that she wouldn't take in her stride.

'Well,' he said tentatively, 'what's it to be?'

'A walk in the park,' Emma said firmly.

'Nothing more?'

'Nothing more.'

She was relieved when he accepted this. He said, as they strolled along beside the lake in St James's Park, pausing to watch the ducks and wild fowl splashing and diving for pieces of bread passers-by were throwing them,

'If I didn't find you so attractive I would have kissed your hand and bade you a polite goodbye when we left the Corner House.'

Emma's heartbeats quickened. How different he was from the other young men she knew! How different he looked, for that matter! She had believed she disliked hippies with long hair and sloppy clothes. And yet at the same time she had sympathy for the students who so much resented the conventional, who leaned towards the Left, who wanted to put the world to rights, who were so convinced that practically everything in it was wrong. She too, she now realized, had ideas and ideals.

He said when she finally said firmly that she must think about going home, 'When can I see you again?'

She hesitated.

'I must — ' he insisted. 'I want to so much. Do you often come to London from your little country vicarage?'

'Not very often.'

'But you can? You are not kept under lock and key?'

She laughed. 'Of course not. My parents let me do very much as I like.'

Even as Emma said this, and she believed it to be true, she was by no means sure that they would approve of her seeing much of Nicky Stagger. But she knew she wanted to see him again.

'I might manage to come next Saturday.'

'You do that. What station do you come to? I'll meet you.'

'No, let's meet at the Corner House. I may come up in the morning and do some shopping.'

It wasn't Emma's real reason for suggesting this. But there might be someone she knew on the train from her village, someone who would say to her mother or father: 'I saw Emma being met by the most extraordinary-looking young man when we travelled up to Town together the other day.'

'In that case couldn't we lunch together?'

'No, let's meet in the afternoon. Something may crop up that will mean, after all, I can't make it till then.'

'O.K. Anyway, I'll call you during the week. Let me make a note of your address and phone number now and you make a note of mine.'

They sat on the grass and exchanged addresses and telephone numbers, though Emma wasn't altogether happy about this. If Nicky phoned her and either of her parents answered how would she explain him? She certainly couldn't tell them the truth, and she didn't want to have to lie to them. Still, she would meet that fence when she came to it.

But in order not to reach it too soon she said, 'I think really it would be better if you didn't phone me. I know I said my parents let me do very much as I like, but . . . ' She hesitated.

'You mean they would want us to have been formally introduced.' Nicky laughed. 'How deliciously old-world.'

Rather to Emma's relief he didn't

pursue the subject. Now he was off again on his favourite hobby-horse. Himself. She only vaguely understood what he was talking about, but as he didn't appear to expect her to contribute anything much to the conversation this apparently didn't matter. He had a musical though thoroughly masculine voice and it came to her ears with the soothing monotony of water running in a brook.

When she glanced at her watch some while later she was astonished to find how the time had flown. She sprang to her feet.

'I must go. I'll be late home as it is.'

'And you'll be told you're a naughty little girl?' Nicky said, teasing her.

'No, but I don't want my mother worrying about me.'

They took a taxi to Waterloo and Nicky held Emma tightly and kissed her as she was sure he would. She had been kissed before, but never as Nicky kissed her.

'Till next Saturday,' he said as he

stood at the carriage window waiting for the train to leave. 'You'll not let me down?'

'I won't let you down.'

As the train moved away Emma stood at the window waving. She wouldn't let Nicky down. She wanted to see him again more than she had ever wanted anything in her life.

2

That was the beginning. Emma met Nicky the following Saturday and the one after that. She had confided in Lucy how he had spoken to her at the Trafalgar Square meeting, and Lucy had listened goggle-eyed and said wasn't Emma glad that she had had to go alone? Emma had said she wasn't sure. The trouble was, it was all so difficult. She couldn't slip off to London week after week without telling her parents of this new young man she had met.

Lucy said she should make a clean breast of things. 'After all, Emma, you're eighteen now, you're of age. You can do as you please.'

Emma had pondered this and decided rather uneasily that maybe Lucy's advice was sound. The trouble was, she didn't want to hurt her parents. She was devoted to them and they to her. But after her third clandestine Saturday meeting with Nicky she decided she must be frank with them.

She told her mother, asking her to tell her father.

'Daddy won't approve, Mummy, I know. I suppose you won't either, but I've got to go on seeing Nicky.' And, with a quaver in her voice: 'I suppose the truth is that I'm in love for the first time in my life.'

Mrs Lawson wasn't entirely surprised by this confession. She had begun to suspect that there could be more in Emma's Saturday visits to London than she was admitting. But she had decided to say nothing till Emma told her herself. Not at least for a week or two.

She was glad that Emma was now being frank with her.

'How old is he, darling?'

'Thirty.'

'What does he do?'

'He's with the foreign department of

the B.B.C. You see, he's not English.'

Mrs Lawson was beginning to feel more uneasy every moment. But she was determined not to behave like an old-fashioned parent. True, she was a parson's wife, but she must move with the times.

'What nationality is he?'

'Krasnovian.' Emma smiled at the puzzled expression on her mother's face. 'It's all right, Mummy. I must have looked as vague as you are looking when Nicky told me.'

'Isn't it one of those small Balkan states between Yugoslavia and Turkey?'

'Yes. I must admit I'd never even heard of it till Nicky told me where he came from.'

Mrs Lawson was determined to be sensible. To try to nip this romance in the bud might only precipitate matters. She realized that Emma was seriously in love with this young man. She knew her Emma. Knew, too, that over the past year or two there had been boyfriends, but none of them serious.

But this was different.

'I think, darling, you should ask Nicky down here to meet your father and me.'

Emma felt intense relief. The news she had just broken to her mother hadn't distressed her mother as much as she had feared. But she hadn't met Nicky yet! And though she was glad her mother wanted him to come to meet her and her father, she was uneasy as to what they would make of him.

'May I ask him next Saturday?'

'By all means, darling.'

'And will you tell Daddy about him?'

'Of course I will.'

Emma looked at her mother anxiously. She was over the first hurdle, but the next one could be higher.

'I don't suppose he's like any young man you've met before.'

Mrs Lawson smiled. 'Darling, I've met a number of young men. Why should I find your Nicky so different?'

Emma spread her hands. She was being wise to warn her mother about

Nicky? She had a mental picture of her own first meeting with him. His long hair and generally untidy appearance. His uncleaned shoes.

'I suppose because he's so unconventional.' Emma smiled as other mental pictures came to her. Nicky telling her how much he loved her, how much he wanted to marry her, telling her about love as he understood it. She heard his voice again : 'Darling, don't you remember that first Saturday we met? I told you then that love and politics were all that mattered.' Of course she remembered. Remembered, too, how he had asked her to go back to his flat with him but she had refused.

Now things were different. Now they were so much in love that they must marry. Even if her parents refused to give their consent, much as she would hate hurting them, she was going to marry Nicky.

Mrs Lawson told her husband what was in the wind that evening after Emma had gone to bed.

'The child's in love, Robert, there is nothing we can do about it.'

'In love with some young man she allowed to pick her up at a political demonstration in Trafalgar Square?'

'Yes. Does it matter so very much where she met him?'

The vicar looked at his wife, amazed that she was apparently prepared to accept the situation.

'Yes, it does. Why couldn't she fall in love with someone of her own sort? From what you tell me, he's a complete outsider. A hippy, I should say, from the sound of it.'

Mrs Lawson sighed. She adored her husband, but there were occasions when she thought he was a little narrow-minded. Which, since he was a parson, he shouldn't be.

'Well, don't pass judgement on him till you've met him,' she said firmly. 'He's coming to lunch on Saturday.'

Emma took the family Mini to the station to meet Nicky. She had tried as tactfully as she could to let him know that her parents were conventional. She was relieved as she saw him step from the train to see that he was looking, for him, almost conventional too. He had had his hair cut, not short as she would have preferred, but at least it was tidy. His sports jacket and flannels were clean, as also were his fingernails.

He smiled down at her. 'Here I am. Ready for inspection. How do I look?'

'Marvellous.'

'Damned if I think so. However . . . Darling, you look, if possible, even more beautiful than last time I saw you.'

'You're biased. Come along. I've the car here.'

'Couldn't we nip into a pub for a quickie before I meet your parents?'

'No, we couldn't,' said Emma firmly.

'Don't you ever nip into a pub, being a parson's daughter?'

'No.'

'What a lot you've missed. But once we are married . . . life could be one glorious pub crawl.'

'Except that I don't drink.'

Nicky's heart quailed. He was deeply in love with Emma, but he was wondering, as he had wondered several times since he met her, how well they would get on together. For assuredly they came from different worlds. But maybe he could make her world his world, or his world hers, which would be far more preferable. At least he would have a darned good try. And if she would meet him half-way . . .

As they drove away from the station he said, 'What have you told your parents about me?'

'You mean, have I told them that I'm in love with you and want to marry you? Yes, of course I have.'

'How have they taken it?'

'Naturally, they want to meet you.'

'Suppose they say a firm no? That you must be mad even to consider such a crazy step.'

'They won't.'

'I hope you're right.'

Emma hoped so too. More than she

had ever hoped anything in her life. Because she was so devoted to them. She would hate to do anything to hurt them. But whether they approved of Nicky or not, she was going to marry him. What the future would hold for her she didn't know. It could be disaster. But she prayed it wouldn't be.

There was the practical financial side to be considered. Nicky had been quite frank with her. He wasn't at the moment earning enough to keep a wife, but if she was game to take a job . . .

Of course she was. Any job. She would want to pull her weight. Most young married wives worked these days. She would be one of them.

They turned in at the drive leading to the vicarage.

'I'm scared stiff,' murmured Nicky.

Emma's hand left the driving wheel and covered his. 'You've no need to be. They're darlings.'

Her parents were on the doorstep waiting for them. Emma said, a trifle

27

breathlessly, 'Daddy — Mummy — this is Nicky.'

Mrs Lawson thought her first impression of this young man who apparently was destined to be her son-in-law wasn't as bad as she had feared. Mr Lawson was reserving judgement.

Lunch was a difficult meal. Somehow there seemed to be no common ground between Nicky and Emma's parents on which they could converse. There were long pauses. Emma realized unhappily how very different Nicky's world, the world which she would enter, was from her parents'. Nicky realized this too. But he didn't let it worry him unduly. Once Emma and he were married she would be away from this starchy environment.

Mr Lawson said, when lunch was over, that he would like to have a chat with Nicky in his study. Nicky shot an anxious glance at Emma, who gave an almost imperceptible nod.

She and her mother went into the drawing-room.

'What does Daddy want to talk to Nicky about?' she asked.

'Well, darling, since you and he are apparently planning to marry, isn't it understandable your father wants to have a private chat with him?'

Emma could imagine the private chat, and how Nicky would hate it. What were his prospects? her father would want to know. Was he in a position to keep a wife? And, above all else, what was his background?

Emma said desperately, her hands clenched together, 'Whatever Daddy and you have to say, I am going to marry Nicky.'

'I know, darling. But you must forgive us for being anxious. All Daddy and I want is for you to be happy.'

'I will be. Divinely happy.'

Mrs Lawson's heart ached for Emma, her only child. How certain she sounded that it would be roses, roses all the way. How very much she, her mother, doubted it. She didn't deny that Nicky had charm, but as a husband he would need so much more. Stability. Unselfishness. Faithfulness. True, she argued with herself, she was only meeting him for the first time, and her first impression had been more favourable than she had expected. But now she was uneasy . . .

'When are you planning to marry?'

'Soon, Mummy. As soon as possible.'

'You're both very young.'

'Not by present-day standards.'

'Why not become engaged and agree to wait?'

Emma said fiercely, because it was something she had discussed with Nicky, 'We don't want to. We want to be married just as soon as it can be arranged.'

A finger of fear touched Mrs Lawson's heart. 'For any special reason?'

Emma leaned forward and kissed her mother. 'Not for the one you fear, Mummy darling. Don't worry. I'm not pregnant. It's just that we are both in love and we want to marry. It's as simple as that.'

Mrs Lawson felt an inward relief. She was almost shocked to find how uneasy she had been. She should have known her Emma better.

A rather red-faced Nicky joined them some while later. Mother and daughter looked at him expectantly.

He addressed himself to Mrs Lawson. 'I am afraid Emma's father doesn't like the idea of me as a son-in-law.'

Emma sprang to her feet and went to Nicky's side and slid her arm through his. 'Whether Daddy likes it or not, you are going to be.'

Mrs Lawson looked from one to the other. 'Couldn't the two of you be engaged for a year or so and then marry — if by then you both still want to?'

Nicky said, 'I do not believe in engagements, Mrs Lawson. In my country when we fall in love we marry.' Nicky almost reproached himself for not having the courage to be more truthful. In his country, when a boy and girl were in love they went to bed together. But this was something his beloved Emma didn't agree with. He supposed it was because she was English and a parson's daughter. Bed, he had discovered to his chagrin, was out with Emma till they married.

Emma pulled at his coat sleeve. 'Let's go for a walk.'

Nicky was relieved at this suggestion. He had had a difficult time with Emma's father. He didn't want to have an equally difficult one with her mother.

'We will go for a walk,' he said, 'and then if you will be so kind you will drive me to the station. I have to be in London by five for a meeting.' Nicky raised Mrs Lawson's hand and kissed it. 'Goodbye,' he said. 'Thank you for inviting me to meet you and Mr Lawson. I am sorry my visit has not been more agreeable.'

Mrs Lawson was as pleased to see him go as he was to be going. As Emma and he left the room her husband came into it.

'That young whipper-snapper gone?'

'Emma and he have gone for a walk and then she is driving him to the station.'

'That's a relief.' He shook his head sadly. 'Has Emma gone out of her mind? She can't possibly marry that young man.'

Mrs Lawson sighed. 'I fear she is quite determined to.'

'Not with my consent, she isn't.'

'I'm afraid she will do so without it.'

'But if I refuse to give it?'

'I am quite sure she will still marry him. Don't forget, Robert, Emma was eighteen on her last birthday.'

'What's that got to do with it? Anyway, it is far too young for a girl to marry.'

'I agree, especially in this case, but if Emma takes the law into her own hands — and I am certain she is going to — there is nothing either of us can do about it.'

Strolling over the fields together, Emma and Nicky were saying very much the same thing.

'Your father can't prevent our marrying,' Nicky said. 'You are of age.'

'I know . . . ' Emma's eyes were full of tears. 'But I would be so much happier if he would agree.'

Nicky stopped, took her in his arms and slowly kissed one eye and then the other.

'I do not like to make you cry, my darling.'

'You're not making me cry, it's Mummy and Daddy.'

'But I am the reason for those tears.'

Emma buried her head against his shoulder. It gave her comfort to feel Nicky's arms tightening about her.

'Would you like for us to say goodbye? Would it be better for you if we didn't meet again?' he asked.

'Nicky, no, of course it wouldn't. I couldn't bear it.'

'In that case, then, the best thing we can do is to marry immediately. We will go to a registrar's office. We will come out man and wife and I will do my best to prove to your parents in time that I am, after all, the right man for you.'

Emma smiled through her tears.

'I know you are.'

'I know I am, too,' Nicky said. He refused to be daunted by the fact that Emma and he were probably very unlikely to be happy owing to their respective backgrounds. All he could think of was that, as soon as they were married, Emma and he would go to bed together.

In the end there was no registry office wedding. With the greatest difficulty Mrs Lawson had persuaded her husband to agree to Nicky and Emma being married in the little country church of which he was vicar, and where Emma had been christened and confirmed. It wasn't a white wedding, because Emma knew that Nicky would hate even to hire a bridegroom's suit. Only a few people were invited. It wasn't the sort of wedding Emma had visualized over the past few years, but all she wanted was to be married to Nicky. And it was some faint comfort that it wasn't a hole-and-corner affair without her parents knowing.

Lucy said to Emma, when the two girls had a moment together during the small reception Mrs Lawson had insisted on giving, 'What's it feel like to be a married woman?'

'I don't know yet.'

'Well, when you do, tell me.'

'I will.'

Lucy's eyes went to Nicky who was talking to two friends of his who had come down from London for the occasion. 'Your Nicky's terribly handsome. I'm not surprised you fell for him.' And reminiscently : 'Funny to think that if I hadn't gone down with 'flu you would never have met him.'

'I know. I've thought that several times.'

'Fate,' said Lucy sagely. 'I've always believed in it.'

'Me too,' agreed Emma.

Nicky came across to her. 'Darling, it is time we were leaving.'

'I'm ready when you are.'

There was no getting out of a white wedding dress and veil and changing into a going-away outfit. There was no honeymoon such as Emma would have liked. They were going to Nicky's little flat in Ebury Street. It would be their home until they could find a larger one, if such a thing were possible. Because it would need to be inexpensive. They were going to have to watch every penny.

Emma intended to look for a job the next day. She would like one in a boutique because at least it was something she had experience in. Madame Barry, who owned the one she had worked in for the past six months, had said how sorry she was to be losing her and if she needed a reference she would be only too pleased to give her one.

Madame Barry had been wonderful to Emma. She had given her the two-piece outfit — an off-white dress and matching coat that she was wearing today — and two other simple little dresses that would come in very useful.

Her parents and the few friends who had been invited crowded round her to say goodbye. Her father had given her £100 and Nicky had hired a car for the day. They had discussed whether they should go away for a honeymoon, but had decided it might be wiser to put the money in the bank for emergencies. Actually it was Emma who had decided this. Nicky had been all for nipping over to Paris for a few days. He could get leave from the B.B.C., he told her, refraining from telling her that it probably wouldn't be easy as he was the only one on the staff who could broadcast the news in his language.

Emma kissed her father goodbye. He looked down at her fondly.

'I hope you're going to be very happy, darling.'

'I know I will be.'

Her father wished he could feel confident that she was right. He very much doubted it. He hadn't liked

Nicky the first time he had met him, and the couple of times since had done nothing to make him change his opinion.

Mrs Lawson held Emma closely and thought of the old saying that in losing a daughter she would be gaining a son. She doubted it. She wasn't so against Nicky as her husband. For Emma's sake she had tried to like him. But it hadn't been easy. She wished Emma were marrying an Englishman.

Nicky touched the self-starter and slid the car into gear. There were waves and goodbyes and Lucy putting her head in at Emma's window and saying, 'Don't forget what you promised to tell me.'

'I won't.'

'What did you promise to tell your friend, darling?'

'What it is like to be a married woman.'

Nicky pressed his foot down on the accelerator and the car gathered speed.

'You will write to her tomorrow and

tell her it is the most wonderful thing in the world. It will be, you know, my darling. I'll do my best to be a good husband, but I know I shall have no difficulty in proving to you that I am a marvellous lover.'

3

Emma soon discovered that Nicky hadn't spoken idly when he had said he doubted his ability to be a good husband but he would make a marvellous lover. He went about love-making with the single-minded absorption of a concert pianist preparing and executing a great performance.

The first few months of their marriage were tempestuous to say the least. There were all-night sessions in smoky rooms filled with long-haired young people, the men mostly bearded and the girls mostly trousered, everybody drinking beer or wine and arguing one another down.

She tried to adjust herself to her new life and when she went home for the day to see her parents, as she did whenever she could, she hid from them that there was quite a lot about marriage to Nicky that she found difficult to cope with.

Nicky never went with her. She didn't ask him to because she didn't want him to have to refuse. She knew her parents didn't ask her to bring him for the same reason. It wasn't a state of affairs that she liked, but it was the only one that seemed possible.

And so time passed. They found a little flat in Fulham, which was more money than Emma thought they could afford, but life in Nicky's one room in Ebury Street had been impossible. And she had been lucky.

The first job the employment agency sent her to proved to be just what she wanted. It was a boutique in the King's Road, Chelsea, which specialized in lingerie, run by a little Frenchwoman of uncertain years with dyed red hair and a face that Emma felt sure had been lifted several times.

She soon found that Nicky had many different sides to him. Before their first year of marriage ended Emma faced the fact that her parents had been right. She should never have married him. It came as a great shock to her when she discovered that he was unfaithful to her. When she told him what she thought of him he looked at her in surprise and she realized that, though he might be a naturalized Englishman, his attitude to women was Continental.

'But, my darling,' he said reproachfully, 'because I make love to another woman it doesn't follow that you mean any the less to me.'

'It means you mean a great deal less to me,' she flung at him bitterly.

He took her in his arms and drew her down beside him on the bed.

'You must not let it,' he said gently. And despite her resentment against him, as he made love to her she found he could still send her soaring in a state of emotional and physical rapture which nothing could ever surpass.

When she went home for the day a few weeks later, Lucy telephoned and asked her if she could go to tea. She wanted especially to see her.

'Do you mind, Mummy?' Emma asked.

'Of course not, darling.'

'Lucy said she will drive me to the station, so I think I'll let her. I want to catch the seven o'clock train back.'

'That's all right, Emma. I believe I know what Lucy particularly wants to see you about.'

'She's not engaged, is she?'

'No. You wait and let her tell you herself.'

Lucy came to fetch Emma about four, driving the Mini family car. Emma kissed her parents goodbye and said she'd see them again soon.

'Next Sunday if you like. As I'm a working girl, that's the best day for me.'

'Who gets Nicky his Sunday lunch?' asked her mother.

'He's got a lot of friends, and on Sundays there are usually demos of one sort or another.'

Emma's mother looked at her husband as Lucy and Emma drove away.

'I'm not a bit happy about Emma.'

'Neither am I.'

'I don't like to probe.'

'Oh, Bob, why did we allow her to marry that awful young man?'

'Because we were powerless to prevent her, as you pointed out to me at the time. Young people come of age when they are eighteen these days and then they can do what they like.'

'It's much too early.'

In the car on the way to Lucy's Emma said, 'What do you want to see me about, Lucy?'

'I've at last persuaded Daddy and Mummy to let me come and take a job in London.'

'That's marvellous,' said Emma, and thought how good it would be to have Lucy in London. She was so short of friends there, and Lucy and she had always got on well together. 'Have you got a job yet?'

'Yes, in the Kensington Library, and I start next Monday. I won't be far from you there, will I, now that you are in

Fulham? I'm staying, to begin with, with Aunt Alice and Uncle Tom, but I'd prefer to be in digs. It was hard enough to get Mummy to agree to let me go to London at all, so I didn't dare say I'd rather be on my own.'

'Well, it's one step in the right direction to be allowed to come to Town.' Emma had met Lucy's uncle and aunt and remembered them as being rather starchy. 'Lucy, I *am* glad you are coming. Let's see lots of each other. Perhaps we can go round some of the art galleries. I used to enjoy them, but Nicky won't come with me and it's not much fun going alone.'

'He's not been down since you've been married. Why is that?'

'To be honest, I don't think Mummy and Daddy like him, and he certainly doesn't like them.'

'That's a shame. I think your parents are dears.'

'So do I, but they and Nicky don't speak the same language.'

'But you and Nicky do, I take it.

You're happy with him, aren't you, Emma?'

'Oh, yes,' Emma said, and hoped her voice carried conviction. When Lucy was in London and they were in constant touch she would probably confide in her and tell her that Nicky and she didn't get on half so well as she had hoped.

At tea Lucy's mother said, 'I'm agreeing to Lucy going to London, Emma, because you are there and I hope you will keep an eye on her.'

'Of course I will, Mrs Brent.'

'I thought that was Uncle Tom's job, aided by Aunt Alice,' said Lucy.

'So it is, but I like to know Emma is there too. After all, she's your own age.'

'Very nearly,' said Lucy, who was six months younger than Emma.

Lucy drove Emma to the station to catch the seven o'clock train.

'I really am quite thrilled at the prospect of starting my job at the Kensington Library and living in London.'

'I'm thrilled at the prospect of you coming there. We'll see lots of each other, I hope. You must come and see Nicky and me. I'll cook you a nice little dinner just as soon as you can.'

'That will have to be next week. I suppose I'll need to be in to dinner on Monday out of courtesy to Aunt and Uncle, but I'd love to come on Tuesday.'

'So you shall.'

'I hope your Nicky will like me when we meet again. He hasn't seen me since your wedding.'

'Of course he will,' Emma said, and hoped she was speaking the truth, but Nicky was so unpredictable. He was also extremely possessive of her and quite clearly believed there should be one law for himself and another for her.

She told Nicky when he came into the flat around ten o'clock that night that Lucy was coming to London.

'Lucy? Should I know who she is?'

'You met her at our wedding. She's

very pretty, so she should appeal to you.'

'If you mean the girl I think you do, I thought she was particularly plain. No sex appeal.'

Emma smiled. She was determined not to quarrel with Nicky over Lucy.

'You have got a one-track mind. Anyway, she's coming to dinner with us on Tuesday.'

Nicky said when the post came the next morning and there was a letter for him from Krasnovia: 'This is pleasant. My cousin Irena is coming to London for her vacation. This is a letter from my father asking me to show her around.'

'I didn't know you had a cousin Irena.'

'I don't tell you everything, darling.'

'You certainly don't,' agreed Emma. But she didn't want to antagonize Nicky, who seemed in an agreeable mood this morning. 'When is she coming?'

'On Thursday.'

'A pity it isn't tomorrow, she could have come to dinner with Lucy.'

'That girl! I'd forgotten she was going to be in London.'

'She came yesterday,' Emma said, for Lucy had called her to say she had arrived and could they meet for a cheap lunch today, a request with which Emma willingly complied.

'I hope she's not going to be always hanging round your neck,' said Nicky.

'Of course she won't be,' Emma said reassuringly. 'You'll be in tomorrow evening for dinner, won't you, Nicky?'

'Do you want me to be?'

'Yes, and I want you to be nice to Lucy.'

'I'll try. And you for your part must be nice to Irena when she comes.'

'I will be. What's she do, by the way?'

'She's a student of economics at Traj University.'

Another intellectual, thought Emma unhappily. She had had her fill of them since her marriage.

Nicky was in to dinner when Lucy came the following evening. Emma wished he hadn't been. Far from being

50

nice to Lucy, he was querulous and almost downright rude to her.

He asked Lucy all the things that Emma knew she couldn't answer with ease. What did she think of the state of the world in general and England in particular? Emma doubted if Lucy had ever given either much thought.

'Have you read Karl Marx?' asked Nicky.

'No.'

'You should. Everyone should. He would show you that there is only one way of life, and that is communism.'

Emma grew increasingly embarrassed.

'Couldn't we talk of something more light-hearted, Nicky? I've asked Lucy here for a gay little dinner.'

'I don't believe in gay little dinners.'

Emma was thankful when, dinner over, Nicky said he had to go out to meet a couple of friends in a pub near by.

'Goodbye, Lucy,' he said. 'See you again some time, I expect.'

'I expect so.'

Neither of the girls spoke till they heard the flat door bang and they knew that Nicky was out of earshot.

Emma looked at Lucy. 'Oh, Lucy, I'm sorry about this. Nicky behaved abominably.'

'Don't worry about me. But *I'm* worrying about *you*. I had an uneasy feeling that your marriage could be going on the rocks, but I thought you would have told me if it had been.'

'We've not seen much of each other lately. I can't tell you how delighted I am that you are here in London and we can meet frequently. I've had nobody to talk to about Nicky. He's not always as he was this evening. We still have happy times together occasionally. You saw him at his worst.'

'I don't think you'd better ask me again. He's quite clearly taken against me.'

Emma sighed. 'It's not you. It's everyone I'm fond of. He's terribly possessive.'

Emma and Lucy were now washing up together in the tiny kitchen.

'I don't want my parents to know,' Emma said. 'You won't give them any idea that all isn't a bed of roses.'

'I won't give a hint of it, I promise you. But I would imagine they must be wondering a little why Nicky never goes down with you to see them. After all, it would be the natural thing for him to do, surely?'

'Actually I've told them Nicky usually has political meetings and demos at the week-ends. Which happens to be true.' Emma gave a wan smile. 'Oh, Lucy, if only you had been with me on that fateful Saturday afternoon — I suppose I'd still be sitting at home, going out to the little boutique — How I wish we could put the clock back.'

Meeting for lunch the next day in a little café which though cheap was quite pleasant, Lucy said : 'How are things?'

Emma shrugged.

'And that means — ?' asked Lucy.

Emma had awakened almost regretting having been so frank with Lucy last night. She had certainly been disloyal to Nicky. Against that, Lucy was her closest friend. And she had so desperately needed someone to talk to. But she wasn't going to tell Lucy of the bitter row Nicky and she had had when he had eventually returned to the flat. A row that had continued when they both got up that morning. She had reproached him for being so rude to Lucy, and he had said she was just a dull little English girl and he hoped Emma wouldn't ask her to the flat any more.

'But, Nicky, the flat is my home,' she had said. 'I'm as entitled to have friends here as much as you.'

That quarrel had ended with Nicky throwing the bacon and eggs at her that she had cooked for him so carefully, and saying he didn't like English breakfasts; in fact, he didn't like anything English, and that included herself.

She had left the egg and bacon on

the floor because, anyway, she was late for her job, and wondered whether he had cleaned it up or if she would return to the flat and find it still there, a congealed sloshy mess on the floor.

* * *

Nicky said at breakfast the following morning that Irena's plane was due to arrive at Heathrow at six o'clock that evening. He had booked her in at a little hotel a couple of streets away and he would meet her and take her there to leave her suitcase and freshen up after the journey, then he would bring her along to the flat.

'Don't expect us before eight,' he had said. 'And have a nice dinner ready when we get here.'

Telling Lucy of this when they met for lunch that day, Emma said, 'Anyone would think I was his housekeeper instead of his wife.'

'Can't you put a little arsenic in whatever it is you are giving them?'

'I don't really think that's much of an idea. Anyway, I don't think that husband of mine is worth doing life!'

Then Emma added seriously, 'What nonsense we are talking. They always say the first year of a marriage is the most difficult. Maybe mine will turn out all right in the end. I'm afraid I've let off too much steam to you about my poor Nicky.'

Lucy doubted it. She had the lowest opinion of Emma's poor Nicky and had decided, after the way he had behaved when she had gone to dinner, that he was the most high-handed, conceited, ill-mannered young man she had ever met. She hadn't been able to understand how Emma had been so foolish as to fall in love with him and marry him. But she was prepared to believe that Emma had been swept off her feet.

'Well, meet me here for lunch tomorrow and tell me how things went. What are you giving them?'

'Melon, goulash and cheese-cake. Nicky's bringing in the drinks.'

'I thought you hated anything with cheese in it.'

'I do, but it's a favourite of Nicky's. I shall just taste a little.'

'Your trouble, darling, is you spoil your Nicky.'

Emma thought Lucy was probably right.

She left the boutique punctually at half-past five. Madame Eulalie smiled as Emma said goodbye.

'You are in a hurry, I can see. I hope it is that you are impatient to meet that loving husband of yours.'

'No,' said Emma, 'but he is bringing a cousin to dinner. She is arriving from Krasnovia this evening and Nicky is bringing her to dinner, and I need to be home early to prepare it for them.'

'Ah, I understand. You wish to show off your cooking. I was like that as a young wife, but — ' Madame Eulalie shook her blue-rinsed head, 'alas, such a state of bliss does not last long, so you must make the most of it.' And then, apologetically: 'But what am I, the old cynic, saying to a charming little wife like you? I only hope you will be one of the lucky ones.'

Emma wished she could be. True, she had said to Lucy that probably things would improve and that she understood the first year of marriage was often considered the most difficult. But much as she longed to believe this, she very much doubted it.

Back at the flat she set about preparing dinner. She had made the goulash the previous evening and it only needed reheating. She had especially chosen a dish that wouldn't spoil if Nicky and his cousin were late.

She changed out of the neat grey dress with its white collar and cuffs that she wore at the boutique into a pale mauve long dress of clinging jersey that she had bought at lunchtime for the occasion. She was glad that long dresses were back for informal dinners at home. She hoped, however lovely Nicky's cousin Irena might turn out to be, she wouldn't outshine her — his wife.

At nine o'clock when Nicky and Irena still hadn't come she went into the kitchen and turned down the gas. The carefully chosen dinner might well spoil after all. To be an hour late was extremely annoying. She wished Nicky had had the good manners to call her from the airport and say Irena's plane had been delayed, which she supposed must be the reason they were so late, but good manners were unknown, it would seem, to Nicky.

At last they arrived.

'Sorry we're a little late, Emma, but Irena's plane didn't get in till long after schedule. Irena, this is Emma. Emma, my cousin Irena.'

Emma held out her hand. 'Hallo,' she said. 'I'm glad you are here at last.'

'Irena has bought us a bottle of Slivovitz,' said Nicky. 'I suggest we have some before dinner.' He took a bottle of wine from a bag he was carrying. 'Just take that into the kitchen and uncork it, will you? It's claret and it needs to be

59

room temperature.'

He ushered Irena into the living-room and told her to sit down, he wouldn't be a minute. He was just going to get some glasses for their Slivovitz.

'You're better at pulling corks than I,' said Emma, handing him the bottle as he came into the kitchen.

'Possibly. I've had more practice, but I can't leave my cousin.'

'You can for the length of time it takes you to pull a cork.'

'Emma, please, don't be difficult.'

Emma was tempted to throw the bottle at him.

Over the pre-dinner Slivovitz, which Emma didn't like at all, she tried to be the polite hostess. But Irena didn't give her much encouragement. She talked, mostly in her native language, to Nicky, and Emma thought she might just as well not be there. And to depress her still more, she had to admit that Irena was extremely attractive in a dark, rather mid-European way. Her eyes were large and dark with thick curling lashes, the skin on her oval-shaped face smooth and creamy, and the only make-up she wore was dark red lipstick. Her figure wasn't so good, Emma thought, as her own. She was on the plump side and by the time she was middle-aged she would be considerably overweight. But now she was voluptuous. She reminded herself that Irena and Nicky were cousins. But what difference did that make? Cousins often fell in love.

She caught herself up quickly. It was absurd in this first meeting with Irena to start imagining that there could be a romance between Nicky and his cousin. Except that she no longer trusted him.

'You can speak English?' she asked.

'Not very well,' said Irena. 'I'm afraid I have been very remiss to speak our language when you do not understand it. But I have not seen my cousin for so long and I have so much to say to him I forget that perhaps I am being rude.'

Nicky laughed. 'Nonsense. Emma

knows that we have a lot to tell each other.'

To Emma's relief, the dinner couldn't have been better even though it had been so long delayed. When she brought in the coffee Irena said, 'You are a wonderful cook. I most truly have enjoyed this dinner.'

Emma turned to Nicky. 'I hope you too enjoyed it, darling.'

'It could have been better.'

'It would have been if you had arrived on time.'

Irena laid a hand on Nicky's arm and said, 'Nicky, you are a very naughty boy. You should tell Emma what a wonderful cook she is.'

'She can be when she likes.'

'The dinner would have been perfect if you had arrived even a little earlier,' said Emma, 'or called me to say how late you would be.'

Nicky raised his eyes to heaven. 'Please, no reproaches. I know you did your best.'

Many times during the last few

months Emma had been tempted to throw something at Nicky, but never so much as tonight. Even more so than a short while ago.

She was glad when at last the evening was over and Irena said she must return to her hotel. She had had a long day and she was tired.

'You must be,' said Emma. 'How long do you expect to be here?'

'About a month. Then I have to go back to my studies.'

'Do you like them?'

Irena shrugged. Her eyes flashed to Nicky. 'Sometimes yes, sometimes no. But this time yes.'

Emma intercepted her look and wondered if she was being very wrong to allow herself to let it influence her. Washing up after Nicky and Irena had gone, she asked herself why she had this deep distrust of Nicky? She knew the answer. She was sure that Irena was a far more serious rival than any of his other girl-friends had been. And though Irena had been pleasant enough to her this evening, she felt the pleasantness had been both forced and false.

She was in bed but not asleep when Nicky eventually returned.

'I thought you said Irena's hotel was only a couple of streets away.'

'That's all it is.'

'It's taken you a long while to see her home.' Emma could have cut her tongue out the moment she had spoken. The last thing she wanted to be was a nagging wife.

'What is that intended to convey?' asked Nicky.

Emma shrugged. He stood at the bottom of the bed and looked at her.

'What was wrong with you this evening?'

Emma leant up on her elbow. 'Nothing.'

'You weren't exactly pleasant to Irena. Considering, as you knew, she was a stranger in this country, I think you could have been more friendly.'

'Don't be ridiculous, of course I was friendly.'

'Oh no, you weren't. She didn't say so, but I'm sure Irena thought you weren't, too.'

Emma sat bolt up right in bed. 'My God, Nicky, for you to talk like this! Not that I was wanting to take it out on Irena in any way, but Tuesday night — '

'What happened on Tuesday night?'

'Lucy came to dinner.'

'That girl.'

'The way you behaved was outrageous.'

'Well, she was a bit dreary, wasn't she?'

Emma picked up her pillow and flung it at Nicky with all her might. She knew she was behaving childishly and exceedingly badly, but she couldn't help herself. She knew, too, that by so doing she was giving Nicky the winning hand. She was letting herself down.

Nicky picked up the pillow and put it behind her head, which she supposed was magnanimous of him.

She turned over, her face to the wall, and closed her eyes, feigning sleep.

One week, two weeks passed. Emma saw no more of Irena and she saw less and less of Nicky. She spent a great deal of time with Lucy, glad to have her in London, to have someone she could talk to. They went round the art galleries together and it was almost like old times. They also spent several evenings together. which, rather to Emma's surprise, Nicky didn't resent.

There came a Saturday when Emma was almost at the end of her tether. She was now facing the hard fact that her marriage was on the rocks. Something would have to be done about it. She couldn't continue to lead this unbearably miserable life any longer.

Lucy and she had been to the Tate Gallery. They came out about seven o'clock.

'Come back and have something to eat with me,' Emma said.

'No, you come and have dinner with

me. Daddy, in a magnanimous mood, sent me five pounds this morning, and I'm itching to spend it.'

'It's sweet of you, Lucy, but I can't let you spend it on me.'

'Oh yes, you can. Aren't you my favourite girlfriend?'

'You're certainly mine.'

They went to a little restaurant in the King's Road. Their order given, Lucy looked hard at Emma.

'Emma dear, what's wrong?'

'You surely know, Lucy.'

'Nicky?'

'Yes.'

'And that so-called cousin of his?'

Emma was startled. 'What do you mean by so-called?'

'Exactly what I said. After all, you only have his word for it that Irena is his cousin.'

It was something Emma hadn't even considered. But now she thought about it, she supposed Lucy could be right. Certainly Nicky wasn't the most truthful of men.

She wasn't sure whether this possibility made her feel worse or better. Now her thoughts were racing ahead. Cousins could fall in love, so really whether Irena was his cousin or not wasn't of much significance.

She looked at Lucy. 'I've been such a fool, haven't I, Lucy?'

'In what way?'

'In marrying Nicky in the first place, and in the second ... well, in swallowing what easily could be a cock-and-bull story that Irena is his cousin.'

'It may, of course, be true.'

Emma shook her head. 'I doubt it.'

Lucy's heart went out to Emma. She could tell her something which she knew would put her in no doubt as to whether Nicky and Irena were cousins. She had been taken out to dinner the previous evening by a boyfriend, one of whom her Aunt Alice and Uncle Tom luckily approved or she would never have been allowed to go. Sitting in a restaurant a few tables away was Nicky with a girl she had judged, going on Emma's description of her, to be Irena. They seemed utterly absorbed with each other. It was obvious that they were in love. When she and her boy-friend left she passed right by Nicky's table, though she doubted, even if he had seen her, whether he would have remembered who she was or that he had met her somewhere. But she didn't propose to tell Emma this. Emma was unhappy enough at the moment without her, Lucy, adding to her misery. But it did help to make her choose the best advice (she hoped) she could give Emma.

Emma said desperately, 'I wish I knew what to do.'

Lucy said, 'I can tell you. Divorce him. You have evidence, surely. 'I mean even before Irena came on the scene?'

'I don't know that it would be convincing enough to make a judge agree that I divorce him.'

'I should take advice about it. My Uncle Tom's a lawyer. Let me arrange for you to see him. He's a pet and I know you'll like him and it will be in the strictest confidence.'

'You're sweet, Lucy. I'll sleep on it and let you know tomorrow.'

Emma didn't sleep on it. She doubted if she slept at all, though she must have dozed fitfully. Nicky didn't come home. She heard a clock striking the hours, twelve, one, two, and then five, six, seven. She wasn't hurt, indeed she doubted if Nicky could hurt her any more, but she was deeply angry.

When at last she heard his key turn in the lock she leant up on her elbow.

'So you've returned at last.'

'That's obvious, isn't it? If this flat were a home fit to return to I'd have been back long ago. But with you nagging me all the while — '

'That's not true. I never nag.'

'That's what you think.'

'Why didn't you come back last night?'

'Because I was at an all-night party.'

'With Irena?'

'Yes. Since she was there and didn't want to leave, I thought I'd better stay around to see no harm came to her.'

Emma didn't believe a word of it. She was completely disillusioned now regarding Nicky.

'All-night parties are all the rage in Traj,' he told her.

'This isn't Traj.'

'Don't I wish it were.'

'If you like Traj so much, why don't you go back there?'

'Because, as you well know, I was deported. But now I'm a naturalized Britisher I may go back shortly for a visit.'

Emma hoped he would. She sat forward in bed, her arms encircling her knees. 'Nicky, I've got to talk to you.'

'Thought of something else you want to nag me about?'

'No. This is serious. Surely you must realize we can't go on like this.'

Nicky shrugged.

'Is Irena really your cousin, Nicky?'

Emma saw a dark red flush creep up

71

Nicky's face. His eyes blazed. 'So that's the latest bee in your bonnet.'

'I'm asking you a simple question. I'd appreciate a simple answer. Yes or no?'

'Okay. You shall have one. No, she isn't.' He glared at Emma. 'So what?'

'Only that I want a divorce.'

'And supposing I don't want one? It takes two to get a divorce.'

'I should have thought you would have been delighted to have one.'

'Well, I'm not and, what is more, I don't propose to agree to one. One day later on maybe I will, but not at the moment.'

'Why not? I no longer mean anything to you, nor you to me.'

'You've got it all cut and dried, haven't you?'

Emma hadn't. She hadn't intended to put her cards on the table quite so bluntly. But now that she had, she was glad. A divorce was the only solution to her problem.

'I have sufficient evidence,' she pointed out. 'You admitted to me months ago that you had been unfaithful to me.'

'Supposing I deny it?'

'Even you wouldn't do that.'

'Don't you believe it. I'll do as I please. I always have all my life.'

'And you've got away with it. But you aren't going to this time.'

'Aren't I? You can't sue me for divorce without naming a co-respondent.'

'I'd imagine there are several I can name, including your so-called cousin Irena.'

'You don't know her full name. Neither could you name any of the others. Listen, Emma, don't be such a little fool. Just take it from me that I don't propose to agree to a divorce.'

★   ★   ★

Emma left it at that. But only temporarily. She decided to ask Lucy to arrange for her to see her Uncle Tom and she would ask his advice. She knew there were other ways of obtaining a divorce. Incompatibility, for instance, and cruelty, though these might be difficult to prove.

She said to Lucy when they met for lunch, 'I'd like to see your Uncle, Lucy. I tackled Nicky about a divorce, but to my surprise he insists he won't agree to one.'

'He can't prevent you suing for one. At least, I wouldn't have thought so, but see what Uncle Tom says. I'll fix an appointment for you.'

Emma saw Lucy's uncle at his office in the Temple the following day. She asked Madame Eulalie if she could have an extra hour during her lunch break.

'But of course,' agreed Madame Eulalie. 'It is the first time you have asked for any time off, so you may have it.'

Emma liked Lucy's uncle, as Lucy had said she would. He was kind and understanding. But he said, as Emma had felt sure he would, that it wouldn't be easy to sue for divorce without naming a co-respondent.

'You say your husband doesn't want a divorce?'

'So he said. I would have thought he would have been only too glad to be rid of me as we are getting on so badly.'

'Perhaps you are wrong. He may try to get on with you better now that he knows you want to divorce him.'

Emma was almost inclined to think this could be so. For Nicky, since that morning she had told him she wanted a divorce, had been much easier.

She telephoned to Lucy's uncle and told him this and said that for the time being perhaps the possibility of a divorce had better be left in abeyance.

4

Emma was secretly pleased when Nicky, a few weeks later, said he was due for leave from the B.B.C. the coming week and he proposed to go back to Krasnovia to see his parents and his friends there.

'I'll be going to Traj. I've not been there since the uprising. It will be interesting to see how it is looking these days. Traj is the capital, as I told you that first day we met.'

Emma remembered a lot else he had told her. How he had been deported for his political activities. She wondered what sort of reception he would get when he returned.

'Is your country peaceful now?' she asked.

'On the surface, but underneath it is still seething. I wouldn't be surprised to hear any day that there will be another uprising.'

'Will it be all right for you to go back there?'

'Oh, yes. I have a British passport.'

'But you were deported.'

Nicky shrugged this off. 'A long while ago. I go this time as a tourist. Nothing will happen to me.'

Emma hoped he was right. Difficult and disappointingly unsatisfactory as she was finding her marriage, she wouldn't want any harm to come to him.

When the day came for him to leave for Traj, since his plane didn't take off till 7.30 she went down in the coach with him to the airport to see him off. She had been a little surprised that he asked her to. But the previous night there had been their rapturous love-making, love-making that dispelled from her mind all the bitterness against him that usually filled it.

When his flight was called he held her closely and kissed her. 'Be good while I'm away.'

She said wryly, '*I*'m the one to ask *you* that.'

'Unfortunately, our ideas of being good are different. In my country — '

At that moment his flight was called. There was another passionate kiss on her lips and he disappeared from view.

She stood irresolutely after he had gone, feeling curiously disinclined to go back to their little flat. Besides, she didn't need to. For the first time since their marriage she was free to do exactly as she liked. Badly though Nicky and she got on, she was always there in the evenings to cook dinner for him unless they were going out somewhere together.

She decided to go up to the lounge with the balcony giving a view of the planes landing and taking off. She would buy herself a drink and watch for Nicky going out to his plane with the other passengers. And gradually it came to her that for a week she would be free. No tension and storms of tempers that with Nicky were so frequent. She could do exactly as she pleased. Determinedly she put all thought of him from her mind. One thing was certain. He would have no difficulty in putting all thought of her from his. As soon as he reached Traj he would doubtless have an affair with some girl who attracted him. He would assuredly not let any thought of her, his wife, prevent him.

★   ★   ★

She had no idea how long she had been asleep when the telephone bell rang. The ringing awakened her and she listened to it, drowsily wondering why Nicky didn't answer it. To be rung up at all hours was normal in their lives. Quite often the B.B.C. called up in the middle of the night to ask Nicky the correct pronunciation of a Krasnovian name or even to summon him to the office to assist in some unexpectedly urgent and important broadcast.

Then she remembered that Nicky wasn't there. She switched on the light and reached for the telephone which was on the table between her bed and Nicky's. A glance at her watch told her that it was ten minutes past two in the morning.

'Mrs Stagger?' asked a pleasant masculine voice. 'I'm sorry to disturb you at such an uncivilized hour. This is the Foreign Office.'

'The Foreign Office? But my husband isn't here.'

'We know that. Mrs Stagger, I hope this won't be a terrible shock to you, but your husband is under arrest in Traj.'

Emma sat up in bed and pulled her dressing-gown round her shoulders.

'Why is he under arrest? What has he done?'

'That's what we don't know yet. We hoped you might be able to tell us something that would throw light on it.'

'I'm afraid I can't.'

'Why did he go to Traj?'

'To see his parents and friends. He hasn't been back for five years.'

'There was nothing political in his visit?'

'Not as far as I know. But what actually happened? Can you tell me?'

'I certainly will tell you all I know, but I'm afraid it's not very much. An under-secretary from H.M. Embassy happened to be at Traj Airport on other business when he saw your husband arrested by Passport Control. He didn't know your husband, of course, but he noticed the passport he produced as a British one. So as soon as your husband was arrested and taken away, our man identified the Passport Control Officer and very rightly demanded an explanation as to why a British national had been treated in this way. He was told that in Krasnovia Mr Stagger was not recognized as a British national and therefore H.M. Embassy was not entitled to an explanation.'

'But that's ridiculous. My husband became a naturalized British subject four years ago.'

'Are you the holder of a British

passport, Mrs Stagger?' the man from the Foreign Office asked politely.

'Yes, I've got one somewhere. I'm not sure I could lay my hands on it at this moment.'

'I'll naturally not bother you to get it at this hour of the night, but when you do find it I suggest you turn to page three of the cover of all British passports, where you will find the following warning concerning dual nationality. I quote : 'United Kingdom nationals who are also nationals of another country cannot be protected by Her Majesty's representatives against the authorities of that country.' Unquote.'

The man coughed politely and went on, 'Instructions have been forwarded to H.M. Ambassador in Traj to make vigorous representations to the Department of Foreign Affairs as soon as it opens this morning, but I am afraid that in this matter H.M. Government has no legal standing and certainly no authority.'

'That's awful.' Emma felt too muddled with shock and sleep and a welter of undefined emotions to recognize what she really thought about it.

'We consider it polite to call you even though it is so late because you are bound to be approached by the press and in such a delicate situation it would be most unwise of you to make a statement which might be regarded as provocative to Krasnovia. If you tell the press no more than you have told me, no harm can be done.'

'I see. Thank you for warning me. I'll be very careful what I say.'

'It might be a good idea for you to call at the Foreign Office some time tomorrow — I mean later today — when we can talk things over. Will you be at home all day?'

'No. I go out to a job.' She gave him the address of the boutique and its telephone number.

'Thank you. Well, we'll call you there. I'm sorry to have disturbed you with such distressing news.'

Emma replaced the receiver, then got out of bed. She drew her dressing-gown round her and went into the living-room and found her passport in a drawer of the bureau.

She read the paragraph which the man from the Foreign Office had quoted. It was just like Nicky not to have noticed it. He was one of those people who never took care about anything or arranged anything in advance. He trusted to luck, and she had to admit that luck was usually with him. He was the only person she knew who could walk into a theatre with 'House Full' boards outside and get tickets without difficulty.

She put her passport back in the drawer and returned to bed. But it was impossible to sleep. Her heart was racing and she realized in a flash of nocturnal revelation that this was due as much from excitement as from apprehension about Nicky.

Why had he been arrested? Could he have been meddling in Krasnovian politics again? But she refused to believe, if this were so, that he had managed to conceal it from her. He was completely transparent where she was concerned. He couldn't hide anything from her successfully.

Or so until now she had believed. But why had he been arrested? Because of his part in the revolt in Krasnovia some years ago? They might not want him back in their country, but why should a small state like Krasnovia risk an international incident because of a harmless, failed revolutionary who had ceased to be of any importance? One thing seemed to her certain: he would be deported again, and very speedily, she imagined.

But supposing he wasn't? Supposing he were put on trial in the incomprehensible way in which foreign nations put people on trial.

Back in bed she found sleep impossible. Lying there in the darkness, with only the sound of a car now and then in the street outside, she began to think about her relationship with Nicky more practically and deeply than she ever had before. They couldn't go on as they were. In which case, why hadn't she accepted this fact and left him? If she wanted a divorce, she had ample evidence.

So why did she stay with him? Sex, habit, and a reluctance to face her parents and admit they had been right about Nicky? She supposed those were the reasons. But he wasn't even a companion for her. One of his Central European characteristics which he hadn't bothered to anglicize was keeping women in a separate compartment of his life. He rarely discussed things with her or took her out. When they had a party, it was mainly his friends who were invited, and the men all clustered together, leaving the women on their own.

At half past five the B.B.C. disturbed her fitful sleep, calling her to ask if there were anything she could add to the press hand-out from the Foreign Office.

She said curtly there was nothing.

Listening to the eight o'clock news, she heard a brief report of Nicky's arrest. As soon as it was over, the telephone bell rang. She lifted the receiver to hear her mother's voice.

'Darling, we've just heard the news. This is terrible. Daddy and I are most upset and terribly concerned for you.'

'I'm all right, Mummy.'

'But you must be so anxious . . . '

'I'm not. I feel quite sure that Nicky will be back here in England this evening. The Krasnovian government deported him once. They'll deport him again.'

Mrs Lawson said she only hoped Emma was right. And then: 'But, darling, why did he go back to Traj if he's already been deported from there?'

'He wanted to see his family and his friends. That surely, Mummy dear, is understandable. And don't forget that now he is a nationalized British subject and holds a British passport.'

'In that case, how dare they arrest

him? I think it's terrible. Listen, Emma, I've talked it over with your father and we both think I should come to London to stay with you until this unpleasant business is cleared up.'

Emma quailed. Despite the brave front she was putting on, her nerves were raw, and, devoted though she was to her mother, she didn't want her to come to stay with her.

'It's sweet of you, Mummy, but it really isn't necessary. You wait. By the time you get the nine o'clock news this evening I feel sure — if they consider it is of sufficient importance — you will hear he is home.'

'I hope you're right. I hate to think of you going through all this alone.'

Emma felt a little guilty at the thought of her mother looking upon her as a loving wife worried out of her wits about her devoted husband.

'I'm all right, Mummy. I don't want either Daddy or you to worry about me. There's really no need.'

There were three reporters and a

photographer waiting for her as she left the flat.

'It's no good,' she said, smiling. She was accustomed to press people because Nicky with his B.B.C. job moved in such circles. 'I have nothing to add to the Foreign Office hand-out.'

'Is it true that you've been asked to call at the Foreign Office today, Mrs Stagger?'

'Yes, that's true.'

'Are you very worried about your husband?'

'No, not really. I am sure he's innocent of any political activities. His arrest must have been one of those routine things. I fully expect him to be expelled from Krasnovia later today.'

They wouldn't let her go until they had taken her photograph half a dozen times. In the end, to get rid of them, she told them she would be late at her boutique where she worked.

'Where is that?' one of them asked.

Caught off her guard, she told them. When she reached the boutique, there they were lying in wait for her on the pavement outside, and a small crowd had gathered to see what was going on.

'This is quite absurd,' she said to them crossly. 'I'm not all that important, neither is my husband.'

But Madame Eulalie, who owned the boutique, was enchanted by the publicity, and encouraged some of the photographers into the shop to take pictures of Emma selling a nightdress to an early customer.

'Isn't it wonderful?' gushed Madame Eulalie. 'Such publicity!' And then, looking at Emma sympathetically : 'But you, you poor little girl, having your loving husband incarcerated in a foreign realm! But the advertisement. Thousands and thousands of pounds in the newspaper could not do more good than this. Everybody will come to my little boutique to see you and when they come they will buy. One never knows with the good God, is it not so? It is all so sudden. Up one minute, down the next. In the midst of life we are in death.'

Madame. Eulalie, when excited, was easily carried away. Emma wished she was less ebullient. But she liked her. She was so warm-hearted. Emma also admired her because she was a shrewd business woman.

It was an unusually busy morning. Besides some unexpected visits from their regular customers who clearly thought that old acquaintance entitled them to a first-hand account of the matter from Emma herself, a lot of casuals came in and bestowed warm smiles on her, even if they were being served by Madame Eulalie herself. But Madame Eulalie was not put out by them.

'For the publicity one has to make sacrifices,' she said, when there was a brief slackening of trade. 'People are like sheep. They will go miles and miles and stand for hours in great discomfort just to look at somebody who was the same as themselves yesterday but today is not.'

'But I am just the same as I was yesterday.'

'Nonsense. Yesterday you are a nobody. Today you are the hard-done-by, heroic wife of a brave man rotting in a foreign prison.'

'He's not been in prison twelve hours yet, so I don't expect he is rotting,' said Emma tartly. But she felt a twinge. Could terrible things be happening to Nicky?

'Have you a heart of stone?' Madame Eulalie asked. 'Do you not love your husband?'

'Madame, please — '

'Ah,' said Madame sympathetically, 'you English, you are so reserved. But I can see that it is the same with you as it was with my husband and me. I have thought for some little while that you were not happy. I know all about it. After the first transports are over — my husband took me to Saint Malo for a week, excursion rates — it was then I saw what a sniffling little swine he was and he ceased to admire my

92

hips. In a year we were separated. He ran away to America with a little chit out of a department store — bargain basement — and I dived into my career.'

'How sad.'

Madame shrugged. '*C'est la vie*. One must beware of transports. But you should be on the crest of the tide and you must not miss the ship. Thousands of people who have never heard of you before will know your name. Your photograph will be in all the papers. You will perhaps be on TV and the radio. *Tiens*. But there will be something already in the early editions of the *Standard* and *Evening News*. We must buy the papers. Jo . . . '

Josephine, who spent most of her time in the back room packing and unpacking lingerie, was a teenager who favoured candy-floss hair and the mini-est of mini skirts. She came hurrying to answer Madame's call.

'Jo, go and fetch the early editions of the evening papers.'

Madame Eulalie continued conversing during any minute in which the boutique happened to be empty.

'Sheeps and foolishness,' she said, lovingly arranging one of her padded bras on a plastic model which stood on a glass-topped counter. 'But we must thank the good God for it or many thousands of excellent people would be out of work. Was there ever an invention more stupid than the padded bra? As soon as a woman wins she must also lose. She lures a man with her beautiful figure, but when he makes love to her where is the figure? Hanging on the back of a chair.'

'But surely a man doesn't marry a woman for her figure?'

Jo came back with the papers, which Madame Eulalie took eagerly. She beamed all over her face.

'Behold,' she said a few moments later, and with a dramatic fingernail stabbed an item at the foot of the front page of the *Standard*. 'No headlines.' Her voice was outraged. 'But I expect the news came too late in the night. Headlines will be tomorrow.'

'I don't expect so,' Emma said. 'Nicky will probably be home by then.'

'You must learn to enjoy your misfortunes,' Madame admonished her. 'It is the only way. But here is a sweet thing which explains the good business. Listen. 'Mrs Stagger, who did not accompany her husband to Traj, is employed in a well-known boutique in King's Road, Chelsea, which specializes in lingerie.''

The reporter, thought Emma, had probably been somebody who knew Nicky, and perhaps her too. He might easily have been at a party they too were at.

'Of course there must be headlines,' Madame Eulalie said. 'Whenever somebody is arrested in a foreign country there are headlines. But what of the B.B.C.? Should they not have sent for you?'

'No, of course not. They know where I am and can contact me if they want to. As Nicky is one of their employees there are probably high-level confer-ences going on to decide how to handle the news of his arrest.'

Madame Eulalie stared at Emma.

'What is going on in your mind? Such anxiety, such turbulence! Even if you are married to a swine, as most of us are, it is the beautiful nature of woman to spill out the soul and the heart's blood even if it is not deserved. But there you stand, so cool and non-attached. It is remarkable.'

'There is nothing going on in my mind,' Emma said, and it was true.

At about eleven o'clock the B.B.C. telephoned to ask if she could go to Broadcasting House to be interviewed for the 'World at One'. She put her hand over the mouthpiece and turned to ask her employer.

'No,' said Madame in a conspiratorial whisper. 'Say you are too busy and they must come here. That will be better.'

So the B.B.C. sent a man and a girl with a tape-recorder and the interview took place in Jo's back room while in the boutique Madame talked at the top of her voice, hoping, Emma felt certain, that some of it would be recorded on the tape.

'Be sure to call us when you've seen the Foreign Office,' said the girl when the interview ended. 'If the story builds up during the day, we may want some more from you, and I expect TV will be on your tail too.'

'Could I put a call through to my parents?' Emma asked when the interview was over. 'They live in Sussex. My mother rang me this morning after she'd heard the eight o'clock news and she sounded rather anxious about me.'

'But of course,' said Madame. 'Naturally they are worried out of their wits. What loving parents wouldn't be?'

Emma was glad that it was her father who answered the telephone. She told him briefly what had been happening and assured him neither he nor her mother had any need to worry about her.

'I know, child, that's what I keep telling your mother. As Nicholas is a naturalized British subject, I'm sure these Krasnovian people will move cautiously and make certain everything's legal. But I'm afraid they may detain him in prison for a week or two. These affairs usually move slowly. I suppose, if it drags on, you may have to go to Traj and try to see him. As a British subject by birth, you would be safe enough, but I'd consult the Foreign Office about it first.'

It hadn't occurred to Emma that she might go to Traj, but when the Foreign Office called her that afternoon asking her to go to see them, this project was suggested.

The room they saw her in was like a room in an ancient stuffy club or an out-of-date hotel in a country town. Chairs and armchairs were upholstered in faded red leather. Immense oil paintings of long-deceased notabilities hung in gilt frames on the panelled walls. The carpet seemed to be about three inches thick, and there was an immense mahogany table which looked as if it might weigh a ton. Tall windows looked out over the trees and green of the park.

She was interviewed — grilled was the word she used when she had the opportunity to think about it afterwards — by a tall, bald-headed, middle-aged man who was introduced as Sir Henry Somebody-or-other, but at the beginning she was so flustered that she forgot his name in a few seconds. With extreme courtesy and extraordinary perspicacity he drained her of everything about her life with Nicky and everything she knew about him. The mildness of his manner went far to counteract the frightening savagery of his black eyebrows.

'H.M. Government,' he said, 'is fully cognisant of the danger that, what is a minor matter of no real importance, may easily be blown up to the dimensions of an international incident unless it is immediately resolved. It came about because your husband failed to read page three of this passport or apply to us for any advice before embarking on his journey. And also because some minor official in Traj put his foot in it. You would be surprised how many international upsets are caused because a pip-squeak in one country, metaphorically speaking, makes a face at some pip-squeak in another.'

This was the second time today, thought Emma, that she had been told that she would be surprised by what are apparently humdrum facts of life to other people.

'There is possibly,' Sir Henry said, 'some connection between that and the undoubted historical fact that so much trouble has been caused in the world by men who once occupied the lower rank of corporal. Napoleon, Hitler, Stalin, and others. But I am digressing, Mrs Stagger. Forgive me. Have you seen the evening papers?'

He took them from a chair beside

him and pushed them across the huge mahogany table to Emma. And there was her photograph on the front page, and there were the headlines Madame Eulalie had longed for.

'We must pray,' Madame Eulalie had said before Emma set off for the Foreign Office, 'that nobody swims the Atlantic, that the poor Prime Minister doesn't lose any by-elections and that nobody has had his head transplanted for somebody else's. I do not wish for anyone to steal your thunder.'

Today at least her prayer had been answered. 'LONDON HOUSEWIFE'S ORDEAL' was one of the headlines. 'B.B.C. WIFE'S AGONIZING WAIT' was the other.

'What nonsense!' said Emma. 'What ordeal are they talking about? And what is a B.B.C. wife? It sounds immoral to me.'

Sir Henry laughed. 'I understand it is all a matter of measurement,' he said. 'If an exact definition will not fit across the page in sufficiently large type, something else — not so exact, but perhaps even more arresting — has to be substituted. But you see what is happening? You are on the way to becoming a national heroine. Heady stuff, isn't it?'

'Not to me,' said Emma flatly. 'I hate it.' But she was conscious of the heavy beating of her heart. Though she wouldn't admit it to Sir Henry, it gave her a strange lurking excitement to think that hundreds of people were reading about her.

'In my young days,' Sir Henry said sadly, 'the days before mass communications, an incident such as this trouble your husband has got himself into would have been settled privately by a few gentlemen of different nationalities sitting round a table talking quietly and drinking wine. Nowadays a million complete idiots know about it within five minutes. Out come the banners, crowds march in the streets, and before you know where you are people are getting killed and governments overthrown.

'Now H.M. Government is convinced that the government in Traj is just as anxious as we are to see this incident closed so long as it can be done without loss of face. But Traj cannot afford to give way to London so far as one of our own nationals is concerned, and therefore we have considered an approach from an unorthdox direction and we have taken the liberty of drafting a letter for you to send to the President of Krasnovia. If you approve of it, you can sign it now and it can go in the diplomatic bag this evening and be delivered in Traj within three hours.'

A secretary, who had been sitting silently further along the vast table, now stood up, produced a typewritten letter from a folder and handed it to Emma to read. She saw that it was headed with her address.

To His Excellency, the President of Krasnovia. Your Excellency, as the wife of Nicholas Stagger, I am writing to beg you to give your personal attention to the arrest of my husband . . .

The letter went on to assure the President that Nicky's visit had no political significance whatever and to ask that he should be immediately released. If this was not possible, would she be permitted to see her husband if she visited Traj?

The letter appeared to be quite innocuous, just that of an anxious devoted wife deeply worried about her husband and, as far as she was able to judge, was unlikely to have any effect whatsoever.

She said as much to Sir Henry, but agreed to sign it.

'We will see,' Sir Henry said. 'At any rate, it can do no harm and it offers a face-saving formula for getting out of a disagreeable situation by making a graceful gesture likely to warm the hearts of the great public.

'Are governments really so petty and stupid?' Emma asked.

'Much worse than this,' Sir Henry said placidly. 'You may probably remember how the Paris Conference was held up for months, some few years ago, while a round table was specially made so that no one delegate was given seating precedence over another.'

'I do remember that vaguely,' said Emma, and then asked, 'Will this letter be made public?'

'It will be a very good thing if it is, but it is of the utmost importance that nobody should suspect that H.M.G. has had anything to do with it, beyond of course delivering it to the President in the diplomatic bag. Have some extra copies made,' he ordered the secretary, 'and while that is being done, I'm sure Mrs Stagger would appreciate a cup of tea.'

It now became a social occasion and Nicky dropped out of sight as if he had never been mentioned. Over tea and wafer-thin sandwiches Sir Henry enthused about his time at college at

Oxford and the wide skies and serene flats of the vistas.

Just before Emma left she asked if Nicky was likely to be well treated in gaol in Traj.

'Oh, yes,' Sir Henry answered. 'They have become very civilized under the present régime. I suppose their gaols are a good deal more comfortable than most of ours.'

This relieved Emma of a nagging sense of guilt. She didn't want any harm to befall Nicky; she was merely glad that he was no longer here, though in due course it would seem that he would come back. At the moment he seemed to be not only hundreds of miles away in space, but years away in time.

There were three reporters waiting for her as she left the Foreign Office, and she told them that she had written a personal letter to the President of Krasnovia appealing for Nicky's release. This news cheered them and they began twitching to get to telephones to send through the news to their offices, though fearful to go before it was certain that she had nothing else to add.

It also electrified the man from the B.B.C., who whisked her away to a studio to be interviewed for television.

That night, alone in her room, she watched and listened to herself on the nine o'clock news. The nice-looking woman she saw might have been a total stranger, entirely different from her built-in conception of herself. She never seemed to look like that in a mirror, and did she really talk in that way? But she supposed that everyone must feel like that on seeing themselves on TV for the first time.

After the news a spate of telephone calls came in; except for one from her mother and another from Lucy, they were mainly from friends of Nicky.

Her mother was almost tearful and clearly extremely anxious. Emma had tried to reassure her. She dared not tell her that there was a possibility of her going to Traj.

Lucy, too, sounded anxious. She had tried to ring Emma at lunch-time at the boutique, but the phone seemed permanently engaged and when she eventually got through, she was told that Emma had been sent for by the Foreign Office. As friends of Nicky continued to telephone, she realized how few of her own friends she had left. Her life had been engulfed in Nicky's. Her friends had to be his friends, her interests his interests. She would have liked children, but he didn't want children. She would have liked to continue her old hobbies of looking at pictures in the art galleries, walking in the country and attending way-out film shows, but these things bored Nicky and she had gradually dropped them, for she was no longer happy as she had once been to do things on her own.

The idea of moving out of the flat before Nicky came back began to germinate in her mind. If she were really going to break with Nicky and make a new life for herself, this was surely the time to do it. She was twenty years old, still young, but nevertheless time would soon start running away from her.

What was life with Nicky leading to? It wasn't giving her anything she wanted. One monotonous week led to another monotonous week, one humiliation sketched out the pattern for the next. When he returned they would take up the same routine; it was likely to get worse. Financially she didn't need him. Her wages and commission from the boutique provided her with enough to live on in reasonable comfort.

She went to bed around eleven, restless, hoping to sleep, but she found it impossible. She tried to read a book, but it was no help at all. She couldn't concentrate on the written page. She thought how only yesterday, when she had watched the aircraft carrying Nicky away, she had promised herself the freedom of a week without him. No bickering. No quarrels. Everything peaceful.

Shortly before midnight the telephone rang again. There was a lot of crackling and hissing on the line, then the operator asked her number and said there was an overseas call for her. Then a heavily accented voice asked her if she was Mrs Stagger, and then said: 'Please hold on for a call from His Excellency, the President of Krasnovia.'

Her immediate reaction was that it must be a hoax. Surely the heads of foreign states didn't ring up nonentities in other countries as one might ring up Aunt Jane in Torquay? But before this line of thought had registered, another voice spoke again, a man's voice, but one which was less heavily accented than the first.

'Forgive me this call so late at night, Mrs Stagger, but I was very moved by your letter, and as it had your telephone number I took this to mean that I might call you. Am I right?'

'Yes, of course. I am very grateful.

But, please — are you really the President?'

She heard a chuckle at the other end of the telephone. She wondered what sort of man he was, calling her in these circumstances. As far as she knew, she hadn't even seen a photograph of him and all she had heard about him was from Nicky, who had violently opposed him and his régime. But his voice and his chuckle told her about the man. She immediately pictured him as somebody in early middle age, cool and authoritative, but warm and kind.

'You think someone makes the joke?' he asked. 'I am the President, I assure you. When we have finished talking you will call your exchange and find out where this call has come from. Satisfied?'

'Yes, your Excellency.'

'Please call me Mr President, it is so much easier.'

'Yes, Mr President.'

'And please stop worrying about your husband. Though he is in our custody, he is perfectly safe and comfortable, and he has everything he needs.'

'Thank you. I am very relieved to know that. I have been terribly worried since I heard of his arrest.'

'Please do not worry any more. As for your coming to see him, please come any time you like. You are free to come and go as you please. We have no quarrel with you, Mrs Stagger, and we are not ogres. I assure you that my police will make no move to arrest you, or follow you about.'

He chuckled again and she found herself laughing with him.

'I'm glad to hear that,' she said.

'I personally guarantee your safety. Now why not visit us tomorrow?'

Emma was taken aback. 'Tomorrow!'

'Why not? You wish to see your husband, and there is an aircraft from London Airport which arrives here every afternoon. Come as my guest. I will arrange accommodation and for you to be met at the airport. Is that all right?'

Emma was in a whirl. She was tempted to pinch herself to make sure she wasn't dreaming.

'Yes, I think so.'

'You do not sound very certain.'

'It is only that I am so taken aback.'

'Let that pass. I am inviting you to Traj so that you can see your husband.'

'It's most generous of you. Thank you very much.'

'That is settled then. I look forward to a talk with you, Mrs Stagger. I see you live in Fulham. I know it well. During the years of my exile in England I had a room in Oakley Street. Sloane Square, the King's Road, I remember them vividly and think of them with affection.'

'You would scarcely recognize them now.'

'So I am told. Such changes are sad but necessary, I suppose. Do you know Tottenham Court Road?'

'Yes, of course.'

'When I was an exile in London I spent a great deal of my time educating myself in the Reading Room of the British Museum. When I could afford it, I used to go for tea to a fish-and-chip shop in Tottenham Court Road. There's nothing in the world like English fish and chips. I wonder if that shop is still there.'

'I'm afraid I don't know. There are probably several. It isn't a street I walk down very often.'

'The number of firebrands who have lit their torches in the British Museum,' the President said. 'You should advise your government to close it.'

'I fear the British Government lacks the charming informality of your Excellency,' she said, and was amazed at finding herself the author of what sounded like a sparkling repartee.

But to be talking from her bedside telephone about fish and chips with the ruler of a foreign power was so fantastic that she wouldn't have been surprised at anything she might say.

This time he laughed outright.

'That is very good, Mrs Stagger. We

shall get along well together, you and I. I feel sure of that. But now I must let you get some sleep. I want you to arrive bright and fresh in our beautiful city and enjoy yourself. So I will say good night. From this moment I will look forward to our meeting tomorrow.'

'Good night, Mr President. And thank you for everything.'

'I will have your Embassy informed immediately that you will be visiting Traj tomorrow as my guest and will be under my personal protection. That is just in case anybody starts worrying about you.'

'I think my parents may. They are already very anxious about this whole affair.'

'Would you like me to telephone to them in the morning?'

'Oh, no, that is too much to ask. I will call them and tell them of our conversation.'

'I know what I will do. I will ask my Ambassador in London to contact them. Would that not be a good idea?'

Emma had a mental picture of the telephone bell ringing in the vicarage at home and most likely her mother answering it. She would probably faint from shock to hear the Krasnovian Embassy wanted to speak to her.

'I think not,' she said, 'though it is very kind of you to suggest it. I will call my mother in the morning and tell her of our conversation and that I am going to Traj.'

'I hope she will not worry about you.'

'I'm afraid she will. My mother is the worrying kind.'

I feel for you. My mother, the good Lord rest her soul, was the same. Now I will say good night. And I look forward to seeing you tomorrow.'

The line clicked and buzzed. Emma replaced the receiver. She didn't need, as the President had suggested, to ring the operator to make sure that call had come from Traj. She was in no doubt at all.

Her heart was fluttering like a bird. She seemed suddenly to see most of her life till now like a straight monotonous path between high, enclosed walls. But suddenly the walls were tumbling down.

5

From the air Traj looked like a crescent-shaped toy town with a mountain on one side and on the other a lake that reflected the blue of the sky. On the mountain side there were clusters of pink-washed villas with flat white roofs that stood amidst the dark green of olive groves and the gold of oranges. Between the foot of the mountain and the lake, coloured toy cars rushed along straight, tree-lined avenues with squares and fountains where they crossed each other. Church spires, the minarets of Moslem mosques and what appeared to be pillars and archways of Roman ruins were everywhere.

When the aircraft landed and the door was opened, an oven-like heat came in. It was a great deal warmer in Traj than it had been in London.

The passengers had been instructed

118

in several languages, one of them English, to remain in their seats until told to move, but now one of the hostesses bent smilingly over Emma and said: 'Please come with me, Mrs Stagger. I will bring your suitcase.'

'Thank you.' Emma felt a rising excitement. She was obviously being given V.I.P. treatment and she thoroughly enjoyed it. What a lot she would have to talk about when she returned to London! Madame Eulalie's eyes would pop out of her head. When Emma had asked her if she could have a few days off to go to Traj she had agreed gladly. She hoped it would be in all the papers and on the News that Mrs Stagger, one of the assistants who worked at her boutique, was flying out to Traj at the request of the President. 'The publicity,' she had exclaimed. 'It will be wonderful. My little boutique will be crowded with customers.'

As Emma came down the steps of the aircraft she saw a tall young man in a well-cut pale blue military uniform waiting there. He came forward to meet her. He clicked his heels, saluted and bowed. He was olive skinned and handsome, and spoke excellent English.

'Mrs Stagger?'

'Yes.'

'I am Captain Ramon of the Presidential staff. Come with me, please. My instructions are to take you to your hotel and then to the palace to meet the President.'

Now that the meeting was imminent Emma felt a sudden shyness and almost wished herself back in London.

'I've never met a President,' she said. 'Ought I to wear anything special?'

'Nothing more special than you are wearing now,' Captain Ramon told her, his soft black eyes travelling up and down her approvingly. 'If you will permit me to say so, you could not look more charming.'

Traj in late afternoon sunshine seemed to Emma to be a noisy animated city, its streets teeming with cars, the drivers blowing their horns most of the time, and its pavements crammed with strolling pedestrians, most of the men using one arm to carry a discarded jacket because of the heat and the other arm for a girl-friend or wife to cling to. Petrol fumes and city smells were almost entirely overlaid by the scent of flowers. There were flowers everywhere, not only municipal blooms growing in beds along the pavement edges, but stalls and baskets of cut flowers being offered for sale at the bases of fountains and statues.

At a cross-roads the car was forced to stop because a procession was going by. It was made up mainly of young men and women, keeping themselves in step by monotonously chanting a slogan. Here and there in the crowd large banners were being carried elevated above the heads of the marchers and held steady by guide ropes. Suddenly she was startled to see the name Nicky Stagger in large letters.

'Who are all these people?' she asked uneasily.

Captain Ramon, who had been entertaining her with racy comments about Traj on the way from the airport but had lapsed into a polite silence when the procession delayed them, now smiled at her.

'They are people demonstrating in favour of your husband, Mrs Stagger.'

'But why? What for? What about? I don't understand.'

'A certain section of the community sees him as a figurehead, one who stands in opposition against the established régime. Street demonstrations are no more forbidden here than they are in London.'

'But it's ridiculous,' she said. 'My husband isn't any longer mixed up in your politics. He's been a naturalized British subject for years. He merely came back here for a holiday to see his parents and old friends. I'm certain of that.'

Captain Ramon smiled politely.

'When he left Krasnovia at the time of the *coup d'état* some years ago, he appeared to many of our people as an adventurous romantic figure after the style of your Robin Hood. Such illusions, when there are nothing but memories, imagination and the wishful thinking of a dispossessed minority to sustain them, grow with the years. It is unfortunate that your husband chose for his holiday this particular time when there happens to be a certain amount of unrest in the country.'

The straggling raggle-taggle at the end of the procession passed by and the big black chauffeur-driven car moved on again with the rest of the traffic. The incident was a shock to Emma. She felt depressed and uneasy. Relieved of a feeling of guilt by the President's telephoned assurance last night that Nicky was safe and comfortable, she had surrendered herself to the enjoyment of a glamorous interlude. Everything was going to turn out all right, she had told herself, so why shouldn't she enjoy herself? But what had seemed likely to be a light-hearted adventure, as improbable and exciting as a romantic thriller bought at the bookstall of a railway station, now displayed a sinister underlayer. 'Anyway, I'm no longer in love with him,' she reminded herself. 'He's treated me abominably and I want to be free of him.' But she had no intention of leaving him in the lurch. She would get him out of this situation if it were possible. But that would be that. She was quite determined now to divorce him.

The big black car edged out of the traffic stream and drew up beneath the glass awning of an immense skyscraper hotel. Emma thought in dismay that she could never afford to stay in such a grand hotel. It was as sumptuous as the Savoy or Claridges.

But as she was ushered into the entrance hall by a platoon of hotel servants Captain Ramon whispered to her: 'I was instructed to tell you not to pay anything here, not even to give tips. You are to regard yourself during your stay in our country as the President's guest.'

'How very kind,' she said, a trifle breathlessly, but it was a great relief.

'I'll wait for you down here,' said Captain Ramon. 'Please be as quick as you can or I shall be in disgrace. The President is eager to meet you and he isn't always the most patient of men.'

The lift whisked Emma up floor after floor and she was led into a suite consisting of a sitting-room, bedroom and bathroom, with a balcony outside the long French windows which gave a view over the gardens, avenues and buildings of Traj.

'What goes on?' she asked her reflection as she re-did her face in the dressing-table triple mirror. She felt almost as if she were a stranger living in a strange, exciting world. She ran a comb through her blonde hair and was glad she had got up early in order to have it done that morning, before she went to catch her plane, glad, too, to find time to buy the new soft grey silk dress and coat she was wearing. Not that she needed the coat. She hung it away in one of the many cupboards that lined the whole length of one wall.

She thought of the little Fulham flat that Nicky and she occupied. One bedroom with very scanty cupboard space, a living-room that was small, and a bathroom that she could hardly turn round in. As for the kitchen — it was no fun trying to cook in it. Nicky had always wanted elaborate meals which seemed to her rather out of character, but she tried to give them to him. But not any more. Her mind was made up. She would help Nicky all she could to get out of the mess he had got himself into, but no more than that.

'Only six minutes,' Captain Ramon said as she joined him in the lounge, and they went out to the waiting car. 'I shall not be shot after all.'

'Is it usual to shoot people here?' she asked.

'Very rarely. Those bad old days are far behind us, I am thankful to say.

Most people would like to keep them there. I was only joking.'

The car soon began to climb a road which wound like a ribbon round and round the mountain, and, looking down, she saw again the pink-washed villas dotted among the olive and orange groves. The sweet scent of orange blossom was almost overpowering.

'Is there a Madame President?' she asked.

'No,' said Captain Ramon. 'His Excellency is a widower. His wife was assassinated at the time of the *coup d'état.*'

'How terrible!'

'It was. They were a very devoted couple. It is a miracle that the President wasn't assassinated also. They were driving together in an open car and a shot was fired at them from a roof-top.'

Emma was appalled at this news. And horrified to think that perhaps Nicky had had a hand in the tragedy.

Captain Ramon patted her arm in a

friendly gesture. 'Do not look so sad, Mrs Stagger. You will make me sorry that I mentioned it to you.'

Emma smiled. 'I'm not sad. But I am very shocked at what you have just told me.'

'It was several years ago. The President has recovered from his loss. Look, now we are approaching the palace.'

They were near the top of the mountain. A high stone wall edged the side of the road, and after about a quarter of a mile of this they came to a pair of immense wrought-iron gates, standing open, with sentry boxes and sentries at their doors. The sentries came to attention and saluted as the car passed through into a wide cobbled courtyard, enclosed on three sides by a grey stone building with pepper-pot towers and carved stonework surrounding its windows.

'Here we are,' Captain Ramon said cheerfully as the car swept forward.

He handed her out and led her up

the stairs. At the top, a tall smiling man was waiting.

'The President,' Captain Ramon murmured to her out of the corner of his mouth.

'How charming of you to visit me, Mrs Stagger,' the President said, taking her hand and kissing it lightly.

Emma judged him to be in his early forties. His dark hair was just beginning to show grey at his temples. She needn't have worried about the informality of her dress, for he was wearing a cream summer suit with a brightly coloured cravat at his throat. She immediately felt *en rapport* with him and her shyness melted away. She felt safe and at ease. She was flattered by the warmth of his welcome, which she felt sure was perfectly genuine. His sunburned face, though lined, had a rugged handsomeness.

Captain Ramon saluted, about turned and ran down the steps. The black car glided out of sight under an archway.

'Come along in,' said the President. 'I

am sure that what you need now is a long, cool drink. It has been very hot here today. Was it hot in London?'

'Not as hot as this, Mr President. How kind you are being to me. I cannot begin to tell you how honoured I feel to be made so welcome.'

'But you are a guest,' he said, giving the impression that that must explain everything.

'I hardly know what to say — in the circumstances.

'We have a saying here in Krasnovia — 'Always postpone sadness, but happiness cannot wait'. Do you not think that is very sensible?'

'I certainly do.'

His English was better now than it had been on the telephone the previous night. He spoke it fluently with very little accent.

'Do you like Traj?' he asked. 'What little you have seen of it.'

'Oh, yes, it seems to be a lovely city.'

'So it is. You must explore it. I hope you may be able to stay for a few days

— a short holiday, perhaps. It will do you good. I hope you will dine with me tonight. But first a gossip and a drink. I have been waiting for you. One of the few rules for good living which I manage to keep is I never drink alone.'

'I can't think why you are being so charming to me,' Emma said, 'considering that my husband — '

The President put up a hand to silence her. 'I told you when I called you last night that we are not ogres here, and only an ogre would be ungracious to an attractive woman, no matter what her husband may have done.'

'But he's done nothing,' Emma said. 'I'm sure of that. To me, at any rate, he's an open book. I'd have known if he came out here for political reasons.'

The President gave her a long, smiling look. 'I only hope you are right.'

All this time he was leading her along a corridor which gave the impression of being as long and wide as a cathedral aisle and almost as old and gloomy. She had never dreamed that her meeting with the President would be so informal. Presumably there were guards and servants somewhere, but, for the moment at any rate, they were out of sight. She and the President might have been alone in this great building.

'What a beautiful floor this is,' she said, making conversation.

'I'm glad you like it. I do, too. These are Roman tiles which were found when one of our motor roads was being made. I had them laid down here.'

He opened a door and ushered Emma into a room that might have been in Kensington or Chelsea. The modern Scandinavian furniture stood on a peacock-blue carpet and the grey stone walls were hung with tapestries. It was one of the most charming rooms she had ever seen. She wondered who had been responsible for its arranging and furnishing. Had it perhaps been the President's wife who had died so tragically?

'What would you like to drink?' he asked. 'Would you care to try one of our local wines, or would you prefer a dry martini or something like that?'

She chose the local product. It seemed diplomatic to do so and, besides, he had put her so completely at ease that she felt gay and carefree again, eager to experience any novelty.

The wine was cool, golden, and delicious. They carried their glasses out to a balcony, from which almost the whole of the city could be seen laid out at the base of the mountain, bespangling itself in twinkling lights as darkness came down.

'Tell me about yourself,' he said. 'I saw you on television last night and knew we should get on well.'

Emma looked at him in astonishment. 'You were able to receive the London programme here?'

'Oh, no, no. The film was made available to our broadcasting company and it was flown over. It was a matter of national interest. Do you see the building over there — the fortress with the tower, near the lake?'

'Yes.'

'That is the prison your husband is in. It isn't a civil prison. Don't worry about that. He isn't locked up among thieves and murderers. It is only for political and military prisoners.'

Emma stared hard, feeling guilty again. But why? she asked herself crossly. Nicky had got himself into this mess and she had come to try to get him out of it. Why should she feel guilty?

'You may see him any time you wish,' the President said. 'If you insist, I will even forego our delightful tête-à-tête dinner together and ask Captain Ramon to take you to him now.'

'That is very considerate of you, Mr President, but I accept your assurance that he is safe and comfortable, so tomorrow will do.'

The President gave her a long speculative look which made her feel uncomfortable, for she was certain she had given herself away and let him guess what her relationship with Nicky really was.

'Does he know I am here in Traj?' she asked.

'Yes, of course. He has been informed and not only that, but he has all the Krasnovian and English papers, none of which has been reticent about your visit.' He paused, then added: 'He hasn't asked that you should immediately go to see him.'

She gave an uneasy laugh. 'That's Nicky,' she said. 'He never does the things he is expected to do. But I'm sure he didn't come here with the intention of making himself a nuisance to you.' She remembered the street procession and hoped she was right.

The President's dark eyes watched hers. 'He was a dangerous man once,' he said, 'and could become so again. He still has a following.'

'I know. I saw a procession in the streets on my way here.'

'That's what I mean. It is quite

exciting to be a dangerous man. I was one once myself.'

'You?'

'Yes. I was every bit as dangerous as your husband. Now I lead a bored and lonely life in this ancient mausoleum. In the mornings I study official papers and see those of my ministers who may wish to consult me. Then I walk round my rose garden and sniff the sweet smell of my blooms.'

'That must be a very pleasant part of your day.'

'It is. But even so it becomes a little monotonous.'

'And after the roses?'

'Sometimes I take a nap when I have had lunch, but more often I exchange polite platitudes with dull but influential visitors. Sometimes, when there are none who have to be seen, I ride or take my boat out on the lake. But all the fun has gone out of life. Was it not Robert Louis Stevenson who wrote that 'to travel hopefully is a better thing than to arrive . . . '?'

Emma nodded. 'And you think that is true?'

'I certainly do.' He sighed and shook his head, and for a few moments they were silent.

The scent of orange-blossom, diluted and freshened by distance and the evening air, rose to them from the mountainside.

'Let me fill your glass again,' said the President. 'I want to refill mine.'

'Thank you. It's lovely wine.'

It was also stronger than its taste suggested. Emma was beginning to feel light-headed and completely carefree. This was an adventure and a wonderfully thrilling one.

Leaving her on the balcony, the President went into the room and switched on a table lamp. A few minutes later she heard his voice, and looking over her shoulder saw that he was on the telephone. She could not understand what he was saying, nor did she try to. She found herself looking towards the fortress where Nicky was, but now it was swallowed up in darkness. All she could see was a dark mass against the shimmering lake and a few street lamps set in a line towards it.

She tried to put thoughts of him out of her mind. Why let him spoil what promised to be a lovely and thrilling evening?

Then she reminded herself that, if it were not for Nicky, she wouldn't be here.

The President returned to the balcony with the replenished wineglasses and sat down again beside her.

'Was my husband deliberately arrested?' she asked. 'What I mean is — was there a sort of standing order that, if ever he arrived here, he was to be put under arrest at once?'

'No, nothing like that at all. It was a mistake on the part of an over-zealous official. If things had gone properly he would merely have been questioned and, on satisfying the security people that his visit was a purely private one, he would have been allowed to go free.

Of course, he would have been kept under observation until he left again, but that is all.'

'It was a mistake, then?' she said.

'Don't we all make mistakes at times?'

He said this in such a meaningful way that she started, and some of the wine spilled out of her glass on to her hand. She was grateful that the gathering darkness hid the colour that she felt rising in her cheeks. How much had the President guessed about her relationship with Nicky? She judged him to be a man of deep perception. The very fact that she hadn't been eager to see Nicky as soon as she arrived and, in fact, had said she would wait till the following day, and that Nicky hadn't asked to see her, must surely have pointed to the fact that all wasn't well between them.

'I was right,' the President said. 'It suddenly occurred to me as I went into the room that I was cruel in keeping you from visiting your husband till tomorrow. You must be anxious to satisfy yourself that he is being well looked after. It must have been only courtesy that made you say tomorrow would do. So I have sent for Captain Ramon and he will take you to the fortress right away. There is still plenty of time before dinner.'

'Oh, no,' Emma said, completely taken aback at this suggestion.

'It's arranged. Captain Ramon will be here in a few moments.'

So she drove down into Traj again with the handsome and entertaining Captain Ramon.

Before she left, the President said to her, 'I asked you to tell me about yourself, but we were side-tracked. I shall look forward to hearing it when you come back.'

She was rather silent during the drive to the fortress, and Captain Ramon, divining her mood, respected it and said little.

She felt puzzled and disappointed, like a child who is taken away in the middle of a party. Why had the President suddenly decided to uproot her so abruptly and send her off to see Nicky? Of course, his explanation might have been the true one and he had genuinely suddenly thought that he was being cruel to her, but she found it hard to believe. She had an idea that he had detected intuitively that Nicky and she were not getting on well together.

Traj seemed to be in a state of excitement, but perhaps it always was. As the big black car swept through the crowded streets she noticed that here and there — on the steps leading up to a fountain basin or on the grass beside the road — orators were addressing knots of people, who for the most part listened in sullen silence. The romantic-looking strolling couples on the pavements, who had seemed so gay and carefree in daylight, were now moving warily and were sometimes jostled by marching gangs of youths chanting slogans. In the light from street lamps and shop windows, people's faces looked colourless and they also looked grave.

The car slowed and turned and went on for a few hundred yards and then stopped.

'Here we are,' Captain Ramon said, and helped her out of the car.

The tall, wide, gloomy frontage of the fortress confronted them. She saw the glimmer of water to left and right of her and realized that the fortress stood on a narrow spit of land jutting out into the lake. There was a pale naked light above the great Gothic double doorway, and other pale lights showed behind barred windows set deep in the granite walls.

Inside the fortress their footsteps rang loudly on the stone floors, hollow echoes accompanied them like ghosts along the gloomy corridors and up the worn steps of a winding staircase as a khaki-clad military officer, carrying a collection of keys on a metal ring that was large enough to go round his wrist, led them farther and farther away into the interior of the ancient building.

'I will wait for you out here,' Captain Ramon said in a low tone as their guide stopped in front of a nail-studded door and searched his bunch of keys for the one he needed. 'Don't hurry, but please bear in mind that the President doesn't like to dine too late.'

Except for the barred windows, there was nothing about Nicky's room to suggest that it was a prison cell. It was large, carpeted, and furnished like a bed-sitting-room in a well-appointed block of flats.

Nicky, looking sullen and angry, was seated in an armchair glaring at an English newspaper. Other newspapers, English and foreign, made a litter on the floor around him.

'What do you think you're doing?' he demanded furiously, springing to his feet the moment he saw her. 'These newspapers, the radio and TV. It's a disgrace. *You, you* all the time! Scarcely a word about me.'

The door had clanged shut behind her, the key turned in the lock. Emma stood and stared at Nicky in utter stupefaction. She had anticipated a cool reception, but she never dreamed that she would find herself confronted with a furious Nicky in a worse temper than she had ever seen him in.

'It isn't my fault,' she said angrily. 'I don't write for the newspapers.'

'Maybe not, but you've given interviews. You were on TV last night. And, to cap it all, you've accepted an invitation to come here as the Dictator's guest . . . His guest — while *I'm* his prisoner. Have you no loyalty to me, your husband?'

Emma felt her temper rising. Loyalty! And to think she had come here to Traj out of that loyalty which Nicky was now accusing her of not possessing.

'Do you think it is a nice and proper way for a wife to behave?' he thundered.

'In the circumstances, yes. The President has been extremely kind to me, and it was loyalty to you that brought me here.'

Nicky scoffed at this and said he didn't believe her.

'I don't care whether you do or not,' Emma said coldly. 'In view of the way you are now behaving, I'm very sorry I bothered to come to see if I could help to get your release.'

Even as she said these words Emma wondered if they were completely honest. True, she had come to help to obtain Nicky's release from prison. But now there seemed so much more. Her meeting with the President had affected her more than she would have believed possible. He seemed to be, even on such short acquaintance, everything she would want a man to be. Courteous, considerate, making her feel immediately at ease. She had never met anyone like him before.

'I'm sorry, too, that you came,' said Nicky. 'And as for your linking up with the Dictator against me — '

'That is absurd,' said Emma. 'And please stop calling the President the Dictator.'

'Why should I? That's what he is. A second Hitler — only you with your tiny bird's brain can't realize it.'

'Listen, Nicky,' said Emma, trying hard not to lose her temper and to keep her voice low, 'surely you must realize that the better I get on with him the easier it will be to get you released.'

'I don't want *you* to get me released,' said Nicky bitterly, stamping his foot. 'The crowds in the street will do that for me. They are behind me with this as they were during the uprising some years ago. That one was unsuccessful, but the next one, one that will be coming soon — '

Emma felt a sudden dreadful fear. 'Is one coming soon?'

'Yes. As soon as I can get out of this god-damn awful place and get things organized.'

Emma gasped. 'Then your coming out here *was* political?'

'Of course it was.'

'You told me you were coming to see your parents and your old friends.'

'I know I did. And you believed me. But you shouldn't have done, because I have been planning this for a long while now.'

Emma was appalled. How little she really knew Nicky. To think she had believed he was through with politics, those connected with Krasnovia at any rate. To think that for some while now he had been plotting to return to Traj and organize an uprising.

'Actually it wasn't till I got here a couple of days ago that I found there will be every chance of the uprising this time being successful. I still have a following. The people are behind me. They are overjoyed that I have returned to deliver them from servitude.'

Emma could only think Nicky had taken leave of his senses. And then she remembered the procession with Nicky's name in large bold lettering on the posters. Remembered, too, that the President had told her there was unrest among his people and it was unfortunate that Nicky had chosen this particular time to return to Traj.

'How could you have lied to me the way you did?' she said bitterly.

'It was easy. You appeared to believe that, just because I didn't talk about the political situation here in my beloved country, I had no further interest in it.'

'I was under the impression that England was now your country. If you feel as strongly as you do about Krasnovia why did you take out British nationality papers?'

'Because it suited me to do so. But now I am back here I realize the people have been waiting for me. I am still capable of saving the nation. I failed the first time, but this second time it will be very different — unless you make me a laughing stock to the world. To judge by the newspapers, I might hardly exist. Do you see this?' He held out one of the English papers for her to see the headline : 'HEROINE HOUSEWIFE FLIES TO IMPRISONED HUSBAND'. He flung it aside. 'What unbelievably sentimental rubbish.'

'All right,' said Emma, trying hard to keep her voice steady. 'I'm not a heroine. I've never pretended to be one. That's just newspaper talk. But I have flown out to help you — that's true enough — though I'm wondering now why I took the trouble.'

'I don't need your help.'

'Nicky, do you mean to say you're prepared to give up your British nationality, your job, your home — me — to get involved in some squalid revolt?'

'There's nothing squalid about it. It is something I *have* to do. The people who are behind me — and there are a great number — believe in me. They know I have come back to set them free.'

There had often been times since her marriage when Emma had been inclined to wonder if Nicky were quite sane. Especially recently.

Now he was off on another tack.

'That ridiculous letter you sent to the Dictator. You didn't write that, I'm certain. You never phrased a letter like that in your life.'

'All right. It was drafted for me by someone at the Foreign Office, but I approved it and signed it.'

'I thought as much.' He banged his clenched fist down on a nearby table. 'You belittle me, you shame me.'

'I've never heard such nonsense in my life.'

'It isn't nonsense. You never understood politics. The very day we met it was because you were so careless you had gone to the wrong meeting.'

Emma let this pass.

'What do you want me to do for you now that I am here?' she asked.

'I want you to stop kow-towing to the Dictator and go back to England and stay there.'

'Perhaps I'll go back tomorrow. I don't know yet. I'll think about it. But tonight I am dining with the President and I am looking forward to it.'

'Dining with him!' Nicky's voice rose in fury. 'Why don't you sleep with him?'

'Would you care?'

'Bah!'

'I don't suppose you would a bit. You have so many other women.'

'That is no business of yours.'

'I would have thought it was since I am your wife. But I wouldn't dream of being so rude as to ignore the President's invitation when he has been so kind to me — and to you, too.'

'I forbid you to dine with him,' Nicky stormed. 'That would be the last straw — the very end.'

'You have no right to forbid me to do anything.'

'I am your husband. In my country wives obey their husbands.'

'But your country is not my country, I am thankful to say.'

'I should have beaten you long ago when things began to go wrong between us. In my country husbands beat their wives when they refuse to do as they are told.'

Emma supposed this could be so in a certain class of the people, but she was sure it wasn't in the one she was mixing in.

'I repeat,' said Emma, 'that tonight I am dining with the President.'

'You will be making a laughing stock of me.'

'That might be a good thing.'

She was now standing by the door and Nicky was standing by his chair. There had been no physical contact between them.

'I must go,' she said. 'We seem to have said all that is necessary. Is there anything you would like me to have sent in for you?'

'No.'

'Perhaps I don't know anything about politics,' she said. 'I found that out when I met you. I'm not cut out for demonstrating or anything of that sort. I thought I might have been when first we married, but I soon realized how wrong I was. True, it was fun to begin with. So is bowling a hoop, but I grew out of both. But you, as I've told you before, are the worst revolutionary I ever heard of. You failed last time, as you admitted. No doubt you'll fail again. I hope so, for the sake of Krasnovia. However, though you have treated me so abominably, I don't want to hear that you've been shot.'

'I'm prepared to be shot,' Nicky said, drawing himself up proudly.

'Well, in spite of your wishes in the matter and in spite of everything, including your frequent infidelities, I intend to do my best to see you are sent back to England.'

'Do nothing of the kind,' Nicky bellowed. 'If you do, I'll never forgive you.'

That was the end of the interview. She rapped on the cell door with her knuckles and was immediately let out by the officer in khaki. Had he been listening, she wondered. She spoke to him in English, but he looked so blank and uncomprehending that she felt satisfied he couldn't have understood a word.

* * *

Shaken to the core, she drove back with Captain Ramon to the palace.

'Did you find your husband comfortable and in good form?' he asked her politely.

'Yes, thank you. I am sure he is being looked after very well.'

The President asked her the same thing when she reached the palace, and she made the same reply.

'I'm afraid the visit has upset you,' he said, handing her another glass of golden wine, 'but I'm glad you went.'

'I'm not sure I am.'

'It was not a satisfactory meeting?'

Emma shook her head. She was feeling suddenly so exhausted that it was almost an effort to speak. She drank some of the wine and it made her feel a little better.

She was aware of the President looking at her sympathetically.

'Poor child!' he said gently. 'Perhaps, after all, I should have let you see him in the morning as was originally decided. You must be utterly exhausted after the strain of the last couple of days.'

Emma managed a faint smile. 'I'm all right. Just rather shaken by Nicky's reception of me.'

'I hope a good dinner will make you feel better.'

'I'm sure it will.'

'Now let us eat,' the President said. 'You must be as hungry as I am.'

'I'm afraid I'm being a terrible nuisance to you,' Emma said. 'I feel it is too bad when you are being so kind to me and to Nicky.'

The President smiled at her. 'I doubt if your Nicky has any cause to be grateful to me. But don't let's worry about things like that. Let us hope that our dinner is well worth waiting for. I'm having it served in here. If one is a widower, as I am, without a family, one of the misfortunes about living in a palace is that everything is on a grand scalc. There are three dining-rooms and the smallest is for twenty people.'

He had changed into a dark jacket and put on a tie, but had made no other concessions to formality. Emma was glad of this. How quickly she had grown to feel at ease with him. It was almost impossible to believe that this calm, gentle, amusing man was the supreme ruler of a nation.

He seemed to take it for granted that her interview with Nicky had not been a success, but he did not question her about it. He left her to sip her wine and recover herself in her own time. He possessed the rare intimate quality that enabled him to watch her without making her feel uneasy or embarrassed.

She sat, seething and silent, while two men-servants in livery came in, laid a table for two, and then went out again.

How dared Nicky have taken that attitude towards her? she thought bitterly. The pompous, jealous conceit of the man. As if any of it had been her fault. Could he really believe he could supplant the President? The very idea of it made her want to laugh.

'Ah, good, I see a smile on your face,' the President said as he returned and joined her on the balcony. 'You are feeling better now.'

She laughed more openly and less angrily.

'I've been feeling so incensed about Nicky. But he is equally incensed with me. We quarrelled — or rather he insisted on quarrelling. He's furious because I have come out here and stolen his thunder in the press. But I had no intention of doing anything like that. I have merely been trying to help him.'

The President nodded understandingly. 'I know, but all the same I can understand how he feels.'

Emma looked at the President anxiously. 'Is there the slightest chance that he could supplant you?' she asked on impulse, and immediately regretted the question.

Not that the President showed any sign of annoyance, but she felt it was something that would have been better left unsaid.

He shrugged. 'It's not impossible. As you have seen for yourself today, he has a following. But he wouldn't last. He might leap in for a brief spell, but he would drag chaos behind him.'

'I'm quite sure he would,' Emma said bitterly.

'You may not have studied such things,' the President continued, 'but if you have, you will have noticed that revolutions are usually sparked off by enthusiastic young people, transparently sincere and burningly idealistic, but depressingly naive and incompetent when the fun and the fury, the roaring through the streets, comes to an end and someone has to get down to the dull slogging work of any government. That is when the cold-eyed, hard-headed men who have usually been lurking out of sight in the background move in and take over.'

'They didn't take over from you,' she said.

He smiled. 'Perhaps I flatter myself, but I think I have turned out to be a competent administrator as well as a soldier.'

'So even you were a wild young revolutionary once. Yes, I can see you storming the barricades.'

'I can't claim to be as young as your husband, but perhaps it was my wider experience that enabled me to dig in and stay on top. Yes, it's intoxicating while it lasts, that sort of thing. 'Roses, roses, all the way,' as one of your poets wrote. I drove through the crowds in Traj, standing in an open car, battle-stained and weary, with everyone cheering me, loving me, throwing flowers, handing up bottles of wine, every woman longing for me to be her lover — does that shock you?'

'No.' Emma was tempted to say she could understand it, but refrained.

'England has changed, of course, though not in everything. I often listen to your news broadcasts — those infinitely cool voices announcing catastrophes as if they were prizes at a flower show. I can well imagine a B.B.C. man saying without a tremor: 'We have learned from a source hitherto reliable that the world will come to an end in two hours. This will necessitate a change of programme which will be announced shortly. Meanwhile I will play a record . . . '

'Are we really as bad as that?' Emma asked, laughing.

'I wouldn't say as bad as that. Perhaps it should be as good as that. At any rate, the English people seem to be less prudish than they used to be. Perhaps they don't kick over the traces any more than they ever did, but now they don't mind admitting it.'

The two men-servants came in again to serve dinner, and Emma and the President sat opposite each other at the small table which had been carried close to the wide open windows so that, by turning her head, Emma could look down the dark slope of the mountain where now the lights of the villas shone like sparks among the oranges and olives, and see the criss-cross spangles of the streets and squares of Traj, with the glimmer of the lake beyond it.

She thought that she had never in her life dined in circumstances and a setting so romantic. Then she felt for a fleeting instant guilty and unhappy. Here she was in an intimate tête-à-tête with her husband's enemy, her husband's jailer. Perhaps Nicky had had a point after all. Would it leak out that she was here dining *à deux* with the President and make a laughing stock of him, as he had suggested?

A betrayed wife usually had plenty of sympathy, but because of some obscure twist in the human outlook, a betrayed husband was often no more than a figure of fun.

Emma told herself that was sheer nonsense. She wasn't out to deceive her husband. Though the circumstances might make some people think so. But surely not. Why should anyone imagine that the President might embark on a love affair with a woman he had known but a few hours?

Nonetheless she became conscious of the hurried beating of her heart. She was struck again by the informality and intimacy of the evening. But was it so extraordinary? How could she know? There was the President's side of it to consider. It was difficult for her to judge, for she had never had the *entré* to such circles before. Perhaps they were most of them like this when the crowds weren't there to see.

The President and she did no more than talk conventionalities during the meal. Emma, having had nothing but a hurried snack for lunch and not liking the food the aircraft hostess offered her, found to her surprise that she was quite hungry.

She had never had such exquisite food. It was simple, but so appetizing. Iced melon, followed by a delicious silver-coloured fish that she couldn't identify, cooked in herbs and butter, then a cold game pie with salad, then ices, cheese, fruit, coffee and brandy to follow.

She reminded herself that it was a brief few hours since the President and she had met, that it was probably taking it for granted that they were now friends.

Yet why shouldn't they be? She had warmed to him from the moment of meeting, she liked him as she had liked few other people on such short acquaintance. And she couldn't help but realize that he found her attractive and sympathetic.

They were chattering away again now. He wanted to hear about London, as it must have changed a lot since he was there. But he had the warmest feelings for the city which had sheltered him during his exile.

And suddenly she found herself wondering what she would do if he started to make love to her. The possibility of this happening was so startling that she told herself she was crazy even to imagine for one moment that he might.

Laying her hand on the table, she noticed her watch.

'It's half past eleven. I'd no idea it was so late,' she said, and with a smile : 'How this evening has flown. But, except for the interlude with Nicky, it has been such a very pleasant one.'

'It has for me, too. I hope you're not going to say you must go back to your hotel. Though, of course, if you are feeling tired I won't attempt to dissuade you. I can summon Captain Ramon any time.'

'I'm not as tired as I was earlier this evening. I think I've got my second wind.'

'And that means ... ? You see, though I speak English I like to imagine almost like an Englishman, a lot of your expressions are new to me.'

'My second wind means that I can certainly stay a little longer.'

'That's what I like to hear.'

'I don't think even if I went to my

hotel I would sleep. My brain is buzzing with everything that's been happening today.'

'That's all right, then. You'll find that you need less sleep in Traj than in many other places. It's stimulating like Paris, Berlin, and the East End of London.'

She stared at him in blank astonishment. 'The East End of London?'

'Yes. Perhaps you don't lay yourself open to such impressions. I seem to be rather sensitive to them. When you are back in London, go to Wapping one day and you may see what I mean. I have been in Wapping when the air has tasted like wine.'

The servants carried the table away and left them with their coffee and brandy.

'Let's go back to the balcony,' suggested the President.

He shook up the cushions of her chair for her, went back into his room to his desk, lingered a moment, and then came back with cigarettes.

Suddenly she caught her breath, for

though she wasn't speaking she heard her voice. After a few words she realized that what she was listening to was a tape-recording of her conversation in the fortress with Nicky. Feeling her cheeks burning, she sprang to her feet, her eyes blazing with a bitter resentment.

'What a mean trick, Mr President!' she said angrily.

'I'm sorry,' he said. 'I had to do that for your sake as much as for mine. If you had been a spy you would have been prepared for something as routine as this. So now I know you are not a spy. Not that I ever doubted it for a moment. But I couldn't have let you be in ignorance that I knew what passed between you and your husband. And as President of my country, it was important that I should.'

He handed her a glass of brandy. She took it automatically and it trembled in her hand. Her knees were weak and trembling, too. She felt betrayed, foolish, furious, but most of all tragically unhappy. How could this man who had charmed her from the first moment she met him do such a thing to her?

'Is this how you treat all your guests?' she asked.

'No. But you are here on a rather unusual visit.'

Emma made no comment. Not that she felt equal to making any.

'How right you are about your husband,' he said. 'He is a very bad conspirator.'

Now she felt small and disgraced, like a child reprimanded for doing wrong. And tears were pricking her eyes, threatening to fall.

'Shall I switch on the tape again?' he asked. 'Would you like to refresh your memory?'

'No, of course I wouldn't. But I'm wishing with all my heart that I had never heard of Traj or been so foolish as to come out here to meet you.'

'Please don't be so cross with me. You're not crying, are you?'

'If I am it's only because I feel so angry and humiliated.'

The President looked at her unhappily. 'But surely you would agree that I am entitled to take a normal precaution to protect myself and my régime. And if I tricked you, didn't you trick me first? Your letter which touched me so much turns out to have been drafted by one of your Foreign Office officials.'

'I could just as easily have written it myself, except that I didn't think of it. They had it ready when I went to see them. They urged me to sign it at once, as they wanted to send it off immediately in the diplomatic bag. Was there anything wrong in that?'

'Of course not. Disappointing, but not wrong. However, let me confess that it wasn't your letter which prompted me to invite you here. I decided on that after seeing you on TV and speaking to you on the telephone. When I realized what a charming woman you were I wanted very much to meet you.'

She stared at him. Smiling, he came close to her and put a hand lightly on her shoulder.

'Please sit down again and let us have some more of our coffee and brandy. You're making me apprehensive. I feel as if you might suddenly run away.'

Now she felt ridiculously like a petulant schoolgirl being coaxed out of a bad temper. But she did as he told her and sat down again and took a sip of brandy. So did he.

'It's good brandy, isn't it?' he said.

'Delicious . . . I'm sorry.'

'What about? I'm the one who should be sorry — and I am, for upsetting you. Unfortunate you, innocent and hard done by, puzzled and confused . . . '

'Why do you say that?'

'Haven't I listened to what you and your husband said to each other?'

Once more she felt the colour rise in her cheeks.

'Let's forget that. I feel better now we have had this talk and I realize that was a routine precaution.'

He got up and went into the room and came out with the small tape-recorder. He turned a switch and she heard the soft whine of machinery. She watched him silently, knowing what he was doing. He was letting the tape run back so that her conversation with Nicky was erased for all time.

'Why have you done that?'

'Aren't you glad?'

'Yes. But — '

He drew his chair nearer to hers.

'I have a cabinet meeting at Parliament House tomorrow afternoon. Naturally, all this business of Nicky Stagger being in the fortress and you having come here to try to get his release will come up. It is the first item on the agenda. I shall say I know all about the situation, which I have in hand. I don't want to blow my own trumpet, as you say in England, but they know I always tell them the truth.'

'How kind you are.'

'But you're a very special girl.' His hand covered hers. She felt her heart racing. 'I'm glad this has happened because it has enabled me to meet you. But perhaps you don't realize yet that chance has pitch-forked you out of your comfortable if frustrated and unhappy life, into a whirlpool of international politics.'

'But what have I to do with it? You arrested my husband and I've come here to plead with you to release him. That's all.'

'Unless it's resolved quickly it will become a great deal more than that.'

'In what way?'

'I'm afraid you may soon find out. Those who oppose me have seized on your husband's arrest to whip up popular feeling for him and against me. His arrest was, of course, the stupid error of a bumbling passport official; but it has happened, and now there's going to be the devil to pay.'

Emma felt a cold finger of fear touch her spine.

'What a lot of trouble Nicky and I are giving you.'

'Don't let that concern you. It's just that your husband, as I said earlier, couldn't have chosen a worse time — or a better, depending which side you are on — to make a reappearance in Traj. Things haven't been going well here recently. The harvest has failed three years in succession. We've had to buy food from other countries, and taxes have of necessity increased. The cost of living has shot up.'

'So it has in England.'

'I know that from your papers. This is the sort of thing that happens in most countries at some time or other, and when it does the population immediately blames the régime in power. Give them bread and circuses, said the old Roman, and that is an excellent way to keep people happy. But if you reach into your pocket and find there is no money for circuses you just have to weather the storm as best you can.'

Emma had recovered from the shock of the tape-recording by now, but all the same she felt nervous, excited, as if she were on the brink of something. The faint scent of orange-blossom kept drifting up the mountain like the breath of a god.

'But surely,' she said, 'all you have to do is to send Nicky back to England. It's as easy as that.'

'No, it isn't, Mrs Stagger.'

'Please call me Emma.' She suddenly felt she hated the name Stagger.

He laughed delightedly. 'You're charming — simply charming. I knew you would be. Of course I'll call you Emma. And you must call me Paul. In private, of course.'

'Of course — Paul.' What was she doing? she asked herself. Which of them was making the running? It certainly shouldn't be her. She had finished her brandy. Could this be the reason for her reckless glow? She concentrated on regaining her equilibrium and was only vaguely aware that Paul was refilling both their glasses.

'Why can't you send him back? Deport him, as he has already been deported once before,' she suggested, covering up and making an emotional retreat.

'I can send him back easily enough, and if I can think of a way to do it quickly, before things get out of hand, probably he won't lose his job.'

'Lose his job!'

'Can you really believe that the B.B.C., with its almost neurotic impartiality, will continue to employ in its foreign services a man who has become the figure-head of a revolt against the ruler of a friendly nation?'

'I hadn't thought of that.'

'If I can find some means of getting him away from this country quickly, you won't have need to think of it. But if the incident drags on and builds up, he's almost certain to get the sack and he'll become that dangerous figure — an unemployed rebel separated from his cause and longing to get back to it.'

'Then send him home to England at once.'

'What good would that do? I can ask your government privately to withdraw his passport and I've no doubt that they will. If for no better reason than that they want to keep my régime in power. They don't want Krasnovia to slip behind the Iron Curtain any more than I do.'

He sat in silence, his handsome face serious and brooding.

'To return to your husband, people who know their way about Europe can get across frontiers without passports and if I merely send him back to London he's bound to turn up here again in a short time. He'll go into hiding for a while, then reappear and lead the underground movement against me.'

Emma said spiritedly, 'Surely he can't do that.'

'Don't you believe it, he can and he will.' He sighed. 'No, simply sending him back is no solution now that he has seen for himself what a following he still has. On the other hand, if I keep him imprisoned my opponents will take advantage of it, building him up as the heaven-sent liberator whom the cynical tyrant is afraid of.'

He paused and looked at Emma. 'I don't want to have him shot,' he said.

She caught her breath and felt a chill go through her. 'I most certainly don't want that.'

'It would be perfectly legal. He is a declared enemy of the state.'

'I — see.'

Emma was aware of mixed emotions holding her. She would never have believed that she would be in such a predicament. Nicky, after all, was still her husband even though she no longer had any feeling for him or he for her.

'I repeat I don't want to have him shot. I don't want a return to those bad old days that I so much hoped would have gone for ever. So what is your solution, Emma?'

'How can I give you one? I had no idea when Nicky went off to Traj a couple of days ago that almost within twenty-four hours I would be here too and — ' She spread her hands. 'I'm sorry I can't think of any solution.'

He glanced at his watch. 'Just about this time last night I telephoned you.'

'I know.' She shook her head disbelievingly. 'I suppose this really is happening. I'm not dreaming, am I?'

'No, but if you were you might awake and find it has all been a nightmare.'

'Oh, no, that is quite wrong.'

'You're not regretting you came?'

'No.'

'Neither am I. Whatever the future holds, I shall always be glad that I have met you. That we have had this one evening together. Despite its vicissitudes.'

'I feel like that, too.'

There was a pause. Emma was aware of the President's eyes on her. She hardly dared meet them. She was so afraid hers might tell him just how affected she had been by their meeting. She knew that, if she never saw him again after this one evening, it would be one she would always remember.

She heard his voice.

'You no longer love your husband, do you?' And then quickly: 'You have no need to answer that. I heard what you both said to each other.'

She looked down at her hands. 'I don't know what that has to do with it.'

'To me it has a very great deal. If I had never met you . . . '

Her heart was racing. She felt colour rising in her cheeks. She was rescued by noticing the time again.

'A quarter to one! Mr President, I truly must go.'

'I thought I was going to be Paul to you when we were alone. Has my frankness shocked you?'

'Shaken me, but not shocked me.' Now she met his eyes. 'But I'm grateful for your honesty about it all.'

'Let us always be honest with each other,' he said.

'Yes, please — I'd like us to be. And now — I must go.'

'I shall have to let you. I have work to do.'

'And I've kept you from it,' she said contritely.

They stood uncertainly and looked at

one another. It was very quiet — only the cool night breeze rustling leaves beneath the balcony.

He took her hands. When he spoke again she felt he was deliberately breaking a spell.

'I've enjoyed meeting you more than I can tell you.'

'And I've enjoyed meeting you.' A smile played round her mouth. 'More than I can ever tell you.'

'I hope I haven't worried you too much. I'll do everything I can to avoid making you unhappy.'

When he said good night to her he put his hands on her shoulders and kissed her lightly on each cheek.

'Good night, Emma.'

'Good night, Paul.'

'We'll meet tomorrow. I will send Captain Ramon to fetch you. I only wish I could see you back to your hotel, but in the circumstances I think it wiser to let him do so.'

6

Emma was awakened by the sound of firing. Strips of sunshine streaming in at the sides of the curtains lit the hotel bedroom. The time was ten minutes past seven.

She lay still for a minute, listening, then got up quickly, reached for her dressing-gown, and went out on to the balcony.

It *was* firing. It came in single shots and sudden vicious machine-gun bursts, with intervals between them. She looked in the direction from which it seemed to be coming. It was the lake, and she saw the narrow strip of land with the fortress at the end of it where she had talked with Nicky the previous evening.

Her heartbeats quickened. She wondered what could be happening.

Her suite was on the twelfth floor and from the balcony she had a magnificent view of Traj. Far beneath her were ornamental lawns decked with flowering plants dividing the hotel from the main avenues. People were standing in doorways and leaning out of windows. A jeweller's shop which seemed only recently to have had its shutters taken down was now having them put up again. There weren't many pedestrians and those there were hurried along, some of them stopping to listen and to look back when a shot was fired. Some cars passed. A bus stopped, took on passengers, and continued its journey. Drivers from a taxi rank stood in a group, smoking and talking.

She could feel an atmosphere of expectancy and apprehension rising from the sun-drenched city.

The intervals between the bursts of firing grew longer and at last it died away completely.

She relaxed and began to breathe more easily.

Down in the street the group of

taxi-drivers broke up and returned to their cars. A man whom she judged to be either the owner or the manager of the jeweller's shop appeared in its doorway, looked up and down the street, then started to remove the shutters once more.

Traj was apparently returning to normal. She went back to her room. She was still a little uneasy. She wished she knew what the firing was about. In this mood it was comforting to give herself over to the luxury in which the President had installed her. She wanted a way to escape from herself and the thoughts that disturbed her, and here it was. Last night she had done little more than undress, get into bed and fall asleep. But now she could delight in her surroundings.

She walked about her suite in bare feet, opening drawers and looking into cupboards, admiring the big bowls of flowers that were everywhere, smiling at her three summer dresses hanging lonely in a big wardrobe, and her few oddments of cosmetics on the dressing-table. She seated herself childishly in the chairs, one after the other, swinging her feet in the sunlight. To think that *she* was staying in a place like this! She had slept in hotel bedrooms no bigger than her present bathroom and much less luxurious.

The bathroom walls were faced from floor to ceiling with tiles of pellucid green glass, each one etched with a design of a fish or an aquatic plant and every one different. She pulled the cord of the electric switch and the walls glowed all over with the light from unseen lamps behind the tiles. It was like being under a sunlit sea. The bath and hand-basin were coffee-coloured, the taps gilt. On a table there was a pile of fluffy towels.

Only fools refused the best the world provided if it was offered without strings.

Now she was face to face with her situation again. Were there strings?

None that she was aware of.

Of course, it would be stupid to pretend that the President hadn't found her attractive or that she in her turn hadn't found him attractive. She was here in fact not because she was Nicky's wife, but because she was a woman who had attracted the President.

But why not? Was there anything wrong about that, or even unusual?

But she was still married to Nicky.

The more she remembered this the more she disliked it. She remembered, too, something which a courier employed by one of the travel agencies had told her at a party, which was that the most respectable people were apt to shed their inhibitions and throw their caps over windmills as soon as they got away from home and across a frontier into another country. Staid matrons could then be counted on to lose their hearts to foreign playboys, and chill company directors dance into the small hours with luscious little pieces who would have frightened the wits out of them in Bournemouth.

Sitting in the warm sunshine, swinging her bare feet beneath a chair, she thought about Paul and Nicky, comparing them. They were entirely different from one another in appearance and personality, yet there was, she realized with a faint shock, a similarity between them. They both had charm. Perhaps Paul, too, could turn his charm on and off like a tap as readily as Nicky could. She hoped not, oh, how she hoped not!

She knew there were countries in which a boy's mother and sisters trained him, as part of his education, in the art of making himself attractive to women, believing, perhaps with good reason, that the most valuable and lastingly important thing he could do with his life was to find the right sort of woman to love him and be loved by him. Was Krasnovia such a country? Were all Krasnovian men the same?

Or was there something colder and more calculated behind Paul's evident desire to charm and please her? He had warned her that she had become a political figure. Did he intend in some way to exploit her?

She hated even to question this possibility in her mind, but she could not forget that he had deliberately sent her to the fortress in order to learn what Nicky and she might say to one another.

She didn't want to think about it. She wanted to enjoy herself, not upset herself. She went into the bathroom and ran a bath and lay soaking in it, luxuriating in the fact that there was no need to worry lest the water ran cold and, even more comforting, no need to worry about the electricity bill.

Paul stayed in her thoughts all the time and she didn't attempt to throw him out of them. Now and then some uncomfortable fact popped into the open and demanded to be looked at, but almost immediately it snapped back again out of sight.

Still, it was one thing to feel an overwhelming attraction for a man after a romantic evening, but quite another to consider a deeper and much more serious relationship.

However, she did consider it, for it gave her so much pleasure, even though she tried to tell herself that she must keep her feet on the ground.

All right then — Paul and she had been thrown together by chance and been mutually drawn to one another. That happened to many numbers of people every day of the week. So far as Paul and she were concerned, it was probably the beginning and the end of it. In a day or two Nicky would be released and she would leave Krasnovia for ever.

But though she realized that here and now in privacy and daylight she ought to be able to shrug it off like that, she couldn't.

At length she dried herself, did her hair and her face, then dressed in her favourite of the three dresses she had brought with her.

There had been no more firing, and when she went out onto the balcony again it was to look down on crowded streets relaxed and colourful, smiles on people's faces, and the fat flower women with the baskets of blooms calling their wares on the steps of the fountains.

Her spirits rose. She wanted to feel happy. Now all seemed to be well with her world again.

There was a knock on the door and a middle-aged woman in Krasnovian dress came into the room.

'Good morning. I trust madam had a good night.'

Emma smiled. 'Very, thank you. And how nice to hear you speaking English. I was wondering how I could order my breakfast. I can't speak your language.'

'I was employed in a London hotel for fifteen years. That's why I've been told to look after you. I work in the sewing-room usually and I've never been allowed to look after any of our guests before. What would you care to have for breakfast?'

'What do people in Traj usually have?'

'Coffee with croissants and butter and honey. But I can bring you bacon and eggs or anything else you would prefer.'

'No, thank you. I'll have the same as the Krasnovians. But what about tea instead of coffee? I think I would rather have that.'

The woman smiled. 'I will make it for you myself, madam. I know how English people like their tea.'

She returned, wheeling a trolley on which was Emma's breakfast, with fruit as well as the honey and croissants, and also more fresh flowers in a small vase.

'That looks most appetizing,' said Emma. 'I think I'll have it on the balcony.'

'As madam wishes. I think the balcony in the sunshine will be very nice for madam.'

'Thank you. What is your name?'

'Maria.'

'That's easy for me to remember. I

suppose you heard the firing?' Emma asked. 'It *was* firing, wasn't it?'

'Yes, madam,' Maria answered cautiously.

'I expect you know who I am and that my husband is a prisoner in the fortress.'

'Yes, madam.'

It was clear to Emma that Maria would have to be coaxed to become communicative.

'Then,' she said, with a bright, encouraging smile, 'I'm sure you must realize that I am tingling with curiosity about it. What was happening?'

'There hasn't been much news yet, madam. Only rumours really, but people are saying that some men tried to get into the fortress to set your husband free, but they were driven off.'

'I see. Then they failed?'

'Yes. It wasn't very much and nobody was killed or wounded.'

'So my husband is still there?'

'Yes, madam.'

'Then nothing serious happened?'

'No, madam.'

'Is there a lot of unrest in the city?'

'Many people seem to be nervous and there are all sorts of rumours.'

'What kind of rumours?'

'It's only what people are saying,' Maria answered uneasily.

'But what are they saying?'

'That there may be fighting and a lot of trouble.'

'Because of my husband?'

'In a way, madam. There are plenty of people who think a great deal of Nicky Stagger. He's a hero to them.'

It struck Emma as strange that Nicky, with his tantrums, unreliability, vanities and childishness, could be accepted as a national hero. Then she remembered from the books she had read what a number of heroes in all eras and many climes had really been like and she ceased to wonder.

'Were you in Traj when the President took over?' she asked.

'Yes, madam.'

'What was it like?'

Maria considered this for a moment. 'To tell the truth, madam, all I really noticed for a couple of days was that the pavements were covered with sunflower seeds.'

'Covered with sunflower seeds!'

'In Krasnovia people chew sunflower seeds like people chew gum in other countries. It was against the law to spit out the husks in the street, so as soon as the revolution happened everybody spat them out just to show their independence.'

Emma laughed and Maria smiled faintly.

'Was that all the revolution was?' asked Emma.

'Oh, no, madam. There was a lot of fighting afterwards and buildings set alight, and we had no gas or electricity. There were no buses, either. But you didn't notice much of the violence unless you were right there where it was happening. Many of the streets were closed and you heard shooting most of the time and buildings were blown up.

The dustbins weren't emptied and there were no letters or newspapers.'

'It must have been very frightening.'

'It was. Many people were killed and wounded. The hospitals were full for weeks afterwards, so that nobody with ordinary things the matter with them could be taken in. And there were lorries filled with men on one side or the other rushing about and sometimes shooting. But most of us, particularly the women, took no part in it. After all, we had to go on living much the same as usual. There was food to get and meals to cook, clothes to wash and children to look after, it didn't matter what was happening in the streets.'

'I see,' said Emma. 'It hadn't occurred to me that a revolution could be like that, but I suppose it would have to be for most people.' She hoped there wouldn't be another one while she was in Traj. She doubted if she could take it as philosophically as Maria.

There was a knock on the door and a page-boy came in with two visiting cards on a salver. He offered the cards to Emma and then said something in his own language to Maria.

'He says there are three men waiting to see you, madam. Two of them sent up cards, and the third is Captain Ramon from the Palace, who says he will wait downstairs until you are ready.'

Emma picked up the cards. One was printed with the words: 'Mr George Hopkins. Third Secretary, British Embassy, Traj'. The other bore the name 'Dr Joseph Stagger', and an address which Emma couldn't pronounce. Dr Stagger? He must be Nicky's father. She had never met any of Nicky's family, but she remembered that his father was a doctor.

The page spoke again to Maria. 'He wants to know, madam, if you will see the gentlemen downstairs or up here and, if you wish to see them separately, which one shall you see first.'

'I'll see them up here,' Emma said. 'I think Mr Hopkins first and alone.'

George Hopkins turned out to be a

long-legged, beaming young man with fair hair and a boisterous manner.

'How are you, Mrs Stagger? Glorious weather, isn't it? But it's usually good in Traj. Just a few raw, wet weeks in the winter, but that's about all. A first-class posting, Traj — plenty of fun and games. I do hope that now there isn't going to be a lot of trouble and nonsense.'

'Are you expecting that there will be?'

'Couldn't say. You never know in places like this. At home all we've got to worry about is the Conservatives and the Labourites, and none of them is likely to set up barricades in the streets. I expect you heard the shooting this morning.'

'Yes. What was it?'

'There's been no official pronouncement yet, but it seems that some of the *buyos* tried to rush the fortress and set your husband free. Machine-guns and all. Not that machine-guns are much use against a fortress with walls eight feet thick. But the idea was to trick their way in through the gates and use the guns inside. However, it was badly organized and soon fell to pieces with no harm done.'

'I suppose that is something to be thankful for.'

'It depends which side you are on, I should say. I don't need to ask which side you are on. Naturally, your husband's.'

Emma was tempted to tell him that he couldn't be more wrong. She was on the side of the President.

Mr Hopkins said, with a keen look in his smiling eyes, 'But things are undeniably hotting up and I've been sent round to tell you that, in the opinion of H.M.G., you may not be entirely safe here and it would be wise for you to return to England today.'

'Today! But why should I? I'm under the personal protection of the President.'

'Yes, Mrs Stagger, we know that. His Excellency was kind enough to give us that assurance before you arrived. But in the opinion of H.M.G., he may not be able to protect you or himself.'

Emma frowned. 'Are things as bad as that?'

'I'm afraid they are. Though I could be wrong. But a political rumpus can blow up very quickly in a country like this and, as you're Nicky Stagger's wife, you've become, though quite unwittingly, a part of it.'

'But it's got nothing to do with me. I'm not a revolutionary, nor am I ever likely to become one.'

George Hopkins smiled. 'I'm sure you're neither smuggling arms nor spying for the President,' he said genially, 'but it's what people may believe about you that counts. We would feel a lot happier at the Embassy if you were safe at home again.'

Emma didn't want to go home!

'But I'm trying to get my husband released,' she said, clutching at the nearest straw. 'I don't see how I can run away and leave him in gaol.'

She felt a complete hypocrite because

nothing would suit her better than to leave Nicky in gaol. She thought unhappily how distressing it was that she didn't care what became of Nicky. At one time she had been so deeply in love with him. She had defied the advice of her parents and friends and married him. But now, how regretful she was that she hadn't taken that advice.

George Hopkins shrugged his shoulders. 'You're a free agent, Mrs Stagger. I'm not bringing you an order from H.M.G., but merely advice. I don't expect you've seen the London papers yet. They aren't usually on sale in Traj till after lunch, but we have some sent over on what we call the milk-plane, first thing in the morning.'

He took a London morning newspaper out of his briefcase and handed it to her. She had made the headline on the front page again :

'NICKY STAGGER'S WIFE HAS
INTIMATE DINNER
WITH THE PRESIDENT'

'I wonder who let that out,' she said angrily.

'There are few secrets in Traj and a number of newspapermen. And of course it is to the advantage of the régime in power to undermine your husband's dignity.'

Emma felt colour rising in her cheeks. Heaven knew how Nicky would feel when he read that headline! And her parents — she had only had time to send them a cable yesterday to say she had arrived safely. But today she would telephone them. Paul would let her do this, she was sure, from the palace.

She looked at Mr Hopkins. 'Are you suggesting that the President gave this news to the press?'

'No, Mrs Stagger, I am saying nothing of the sort, for the simple reason that I don't know. But it could very well be that the gossip of the palace servants has leaked into Traj without the President's knowledge.'

That was reassuring. She couldn't have borne to think that Paul had been responsible. If he had been, it could only mean that he had asked her to Traj in order to exploit her regarding Nicky. But even as these thoughts flashed through her mind she rebuked herself. True, she had only met Paul yesterday, but she should know him better than to suspect that.

George Hopkins went on : 'People won't allow themselves as a rule to be led by somebody who can be laughed at. True, Hitler got away with it even with that silly little moustache, but the Germans have no sense of humour. If Hitler had tried it on in Krasnovia he would have been jeered into obscurity in a week. In Krasnovia people laugh very readily. You'll find something interesting on page four, in the gossip.'

She turned the pages with an angrily shaking hand, feeling guilty as she remembered all Nicky had had to say about making him a laughing-stock.

'Traj, which rivals Paris and Vienna in the matter of malicious café wit, had a high old time last night, for while Nicky Stagger, who has suddenly become the figurehead of the underground Leftish party, was behind bars at the Fortress of St Mark, his lovely young English wife was being entertained by the president to a tête-à-tête dinner at the palace which went on until the early hours of the morning. Some of the city's cabaret singers, who specialize in producing up-to-the-minute songs about local and political events, took full advantage of the situation and really went to town. Not only that, but already drawings of Nicky Stagger, wearing the traditional cuckold's horns are to be seen on walls and kiosks all over the city. We wonder if Emma Stagger knows the sort of hornets' nest she may be sitting on.'

She threw the paper down angrily. 'It's outrageous to suggest there is anything between me and the President. Surely it is libellous?'

'Could be,' said George Hopkins.

'But the papers are only reporting what is going on. I was at a Traj cabaret last night and heard one of the songs myself and it's true there are pictures of your husband scrawled all over the place. I've seen them.'

Emma fought against tears that were perilously near the surface. She couldn't help thinking that what the gossip writers had been hinting at could easily have been true. If Paul and she had been a little less cautious last night and Paul a little more reckless . . .

But she hated being talked to like this. How dared an underling from the Embassy do so?

'So you see, Mrs Stagger,' said George Hopkins, 'you may easily be in danger. Your husband's following is building up. They won't relish their hero being made to look foolish, any more than I imagine he relishes it himself.'

'Yes, I understand. Thank you,' she said shortly. 'I'll think about your advice and perhaps I'll go home today. I don't know yet.'

George Hopkins got up from his chair, accepting his dismissal amicably.

'Call me when you've decided about it, Mrs Stagger, and I'll make sure there's a seat for you on the plane.'

After he had gone, Emma gave herself a few minutes to calm down before seeing Dr Stagger.

Am I really behaving badly? she asked herself. It was easy to tell herself that she owed nothing to Nicky, that emotionally and physically she was finished with him, that the ties that bound them in the earlier days had long ago become frayed. But it wasn't easy to throw over the traditions and conventions of her upbringing.

It would be absurd to imagine that there could be anything deeper than a strong mutual attraction between the President and herself. She hadn't met him till yesterday.

George Hopkins had stung her. Yet he seemed a pleasant enough young man.

Was it possible that he had been

carrying out an order, that he had been told to talk to her in that way? And if so, by whom? Paul? Surely not. That was unthinkable. She felt distracted, unable to see the wood for the trees. And where did she go from here? To see Dr Stagger, presumably. She hoped she wasn't in for another unpleasant interview.

Now for the first time she realized that what had been said to her by the President and George Hopkins, and hinted at in the London newspaper, could actually be true. As if by a sudden revelation she accepted at last that what she had been told was not fanciful, but a simple statement of fact. She *had* become a political figure.

She felt frightened. Her imagination coiled round her and she felt as if she were being lapped about by a dark and rising tide of mysterious intrigue.

She went into the bedroom where Maria had just finished tidying and asked that Dr Stagger should be sent for.

Dr Stagger did not appear to resemble Nicky in any way. He was a plump, grey-haired man with a thick body and a solemn, professional face. He clicked his heels and bowed to her stiffly from the waist, then spoke to her in slow and throaty English.

'It is unlucky that my first meeting with my daughter-in-law should be on an occasion so unfortunate. I come from my son to ask that you return to England at once. You are doing him no service by being here.'

'I thought I was. I am trying to persuade the President to release him.'

'By dining *à deux* with him as you did last night?' Dr Stagger shook his head. 'Oh, no, that is not the way to gain my son's release. It will be better for that to come from his loyal friends and followers.'

'It is difficult for me to believe that he can be serious about this.'

Dr Stagger drew himself up proudly. 'Of course he is serious. It is a serious matter. It is not a matter of flirtation and private dinners at the palace. If you had done your duty as my son's wife you would have refused to see the President except at a formal official audience. It is a disgrace that you behave like' — here there was a significant pause — 'like the President's friend. You are a disgrace to my family.'

'You've no right to say such things to me, Dr Stagger,' Emma said angrily. 'There's nothing guilty in my relationship with the President. He's been very kind to me, and in the circumstances very kind to Nicky, too. Besides, Nicky has treated me appallingly all through our married life. He's been unfaithful to me countless times — '

Nicky's father waved this aside. 'That is of no importance. You are his wife. It is your duty to obey him and protect his dignity, not to make a mockery of him.'

'Yours is the Continental outlook. I see things differently. In England most of us still believe that it is important that a husband should be faithful to his wife.'

Dr Stagger would have none of this. 'Peccadilloes only. Here in Krasnovia it is merely of importance that the wife should be faithful to her husband.'

'Do you not consider that most unfair? Why should there be one law for a man and another for a woman?'

Dr Stagger didn't answer this. 'I am not here to argue with you,' he said. 'I repeat, please return to England at once and do not come to Traj again unless my son sends for you.'

'If Nicky sent for me that would be the last thing to bring me back,' Emma said, angry with herself for retorting like a defiant child, but unable to help herself. 'For your information, I intend to divorce him as soon as I can.'

Dr Stagger inclined his head stiffly. 'That is a matter for you and the English law, whatever the English law may be about such matters. But please go to London at once. Today.'

When Emma went into the corridor after Nicky's father had gone, she saw two heavily-built men walking along side by side, and the sight of them sent a shudder through her. She turned quickly back into her suite and locked the door. Maria had gone. She went on rapid tip-toe to the telephone, though why on tip-toe she didn't know except that she was thoroughly unnerved.

'Maria, please, Maria,' she whispered when the girl on the switchboard answered.

'*Yohl*, madame,' the girl answered.

Yohl and *noy* — yes and no — were the only two Krasnovian words Emma had as yet learned.

In a couple of minutes there was a knock on the door.

'Is that Maria?' Emma asked.

'*Yohl*, madame.'

'I'll unlock the door.'

'Is there something wrong?' Maria asked as Emma opened the door to her.

'I don't know. I was just going down to Captain Ramon when I saw two awful-looking men walking along the corridor.'

Maria relaxed and smiled.

208

'They are only your bodyguard — two policemen in plain clothes. They change every four hours, but two are there all the while.'

Greatly relieved, Emma left her suite and went to the lift, giving a smile to the two awful-looking men as they passed her.

Brushed and polished as on the previous night, in his beautifully cut pale blue uniform, Captain Ramon sprang up from a chair in the entrance hall and greeted her with a bow and a click of his heels.

'Good morning, Mrs Stagger. Did you sleep well?'

'Yes, thank you. Like a top.'

He looked puzzled. 'I do not know what a top is, but no doubt it is something very nice. You must tell me. I was to show you the sights of Traj this morning, but now I am ordered to take you to the palace immediately.'

As Emma walked with him to the big black car there suddenly flashed through her mind, out of the blue in the way things do, something the President had said to her the previous night. 'Let us always be honest with one another.'

The memory was a comfort to her and an encouragement.

7

It was good to see Paul again. Though it was only a few hours since they had parted, Emma felt her heartbeats race as they met.

'I was hoping,' he said, 'to let Captain Ramon show you Traj, but there have been developments since last night which made me want to see you at once.'

They were on the balcony again as they had been the previous night. Paul looked at Emma. 'This may be an extraordinary thing to say to you, but these are extraordinary circumstances. I will say no more than that, since meeting you yesterday, whatever the outcome of that meeting may be, it will always be to me of the greatest significance.'

'To me, too,' said Emma.

Paul looked at her. 'You mean that?'

'I never say things I don't mean.'

A manservant put a coffee tray on a table between them. Paul looked at Emma. 'Shall we have coffee?'

'I'd like some.'

'Will you pour out?'

'Of course.'

'My wife and I, whenever I was at home, always had coffee at this time of the morning and she always poured out for us.'

'Captain Ramon told me what happened. I don't quite know what to say, but I'd like to tell you how much I feel for you.'

'Thank you. It was terrible at the time. But one recovers, surprisingly, from even the most terrible things. And' — Paul paused — 'I think you could help me to put it to the back of my mind. And, what is more, I know that my wife would want you to.'

It was an extraordinary conversation, but, as Paul had just said, these were extraordinary circumstances.

'I think you should return to England.'

'Why?'

'Because of the unrest in my country. Did you hear firing this morning?'

'I certainly did.'

'Did it alarm you?'

'I'll admit it unnerved me.'

'I thought it would. The country is in a state of turmoil, largely brought about because your husband is here. I hope when he is back in England it will quieten down again. What I would suggest is that you return on the afternoon plane, which leaves at 2.30. I have already made reservations for you both. Your husband will go direct from the fortress to the airport.'

'I see. If it is your wish, of course I agree with it.'

Paul smiled. 'How easy you are. Many women would have refused.'

'As I am a guest, what can I do other than agree with my host's wishes?'

There was a long pause.

Then Paul said, 'It is not so straightforward as you may think. I want you to do something for me, Emma.'

Emma looked him straight in the eyes. 'Of course I will. Anything you wish.'

'If you find your husband behaving in even the slightest suspicious way, will you let me know? It is possible that, when this present unrest has subsided and your husband is back in England, it may flare up again. He has a large following. I would like to be warned if he leaves England.'

'I will let you know at once,' she promised.

'Now — ' Paul's face cleared, but Emma realized that it was an effort to throw off his anxieties. 'I propose to take you for a drive round Traj myself and we will return here for an early lunch and I will take you to your plane.'

Emma said anxiously, 'Would that be wise? Captain Ramon said some rather disquieting things to me on our way here.'

'I know. I was hoping they would escape you.'

'As they haven't, wouldn't it be more

sensible for Captain Ramon to see me off?'

'You are probably right.' Paul went to the telephone. After a few moments he returned. 'Captain Ramon will be here at two o'clock.' He looked at her sadly. 'I hate this. Your first visit to Traj is far too short. You'll come again?'

'I hope so.'

'In happier circumstances?'

'I hope that, too.'

'I think we should have a code. As we have arranged, I will call you every evening about ten, but in a country like mine one never knows what might happen. If, for example, I were taken prisoner and made to talk under duress I suggest I would say to you, 'I haven't heard from you for a long time.' Then you would contact my Embassy in London and tell them what has happened and they would get help to me.' He smiled and touched her cheek. 'This may all sound like a blood-and-thunder thriller to you, but in a case like this, one never knows what may happen.'

215

'I'll be on my guard,' she promised him.

A manservant came to say the President's car was at the door.

Emma looked at Paul diffidently. 'How long does it take to get a phone call through to England?'

'No time at all if I ask for it. Is there one you want to make?'

'Yes, if you would be so kind as to let me. I think my parents are almost certainly worrying about me. I only had time to send them a cable when I arrived yesterday.'

Paul went to the telephone and gave a number.

Emma looked at him wonderingly. 'You know my parents' number?'

'Yes. I asked our Embassy in London to find it for me in case it should be needed.' He smiled. 'Among other things, I am resourceful.' He handed the receiver to Emma. 'Here you are. Take as long as you like. We have ample time for me to take you for a drive, then we will come back here for lunch and, as you suggest, Captain Ramon will see you to your plane.'

Paul left the room, thinking, Emma was sure, that she would prefer to be by herself.

This time it was her mother who answered. Emma had hoped, as yesterday morning, it might have been her father.

Her mother sounded on the verge of tears. 'Emma darling, your father and I have been so worried about you.'

'You had no reason to be. I'm calling you to tell you I am coming back to England this afternoon. My plane leaves at 2.30 and I will ring you as soon as I reach the flat.'

'Is Nicky coming with you?'

'Yes.'

'Where are you now?'

'With the President of Krasnovia, who invited me to Traj.'

'Yes, I know. There has been quite a lot in the papers about him.'

'Most of which is untrue,' said Emma tartly. 'Mummy, I can't chatter to you

217

now. As I said, I'll call you this evening.'

She replaced the receiver. She could well imagine what was going on between her parents in the little country vicarage. Her mother would almost certainly be crying copiously and her father would be trying to comfort her. The fact that she had telephoned in order to save them worrying wouldn't stop her mother from worrying about her. But at least her father would no longer be anxious.

Paul came back into the room. 'Did you get a clear line?'

'Yes. I might have been making the call from London.'

'Were your parents relieved to hear from you?'

'I'm sure they were. Luckily, my father doesn't panic easily. Unfortunately, my mother does.'

Paul said with a smile, 'Perhaps if I had a daughter like you I would panic.'

If I had a son like you, Emma was tempted to say, so would I.

But it wasn't for her to say anything

like that. She didn't want to be provocative, and that certainly would be. But it was for him to do the running.

What a strange situation it was! Here was she with a man she had known scarcely twenty-four hours and without any doubt she was deeply in love with him. More in love than she had ever been with Nicky. Now she realized that her marriage had been based on sex. And a marriage needed so much more. It needed mutual trust, deep affection, understanding and unselfishness. None of which Nicky had for her, nor, she realized, would he ever be likely to have. To be frank, she had to admit neither had she for Nicky. But she could have had if only things had been different.

She doubted if Nicky was capable of loving any woman unselfishly. He was too fond of Nicky Stagger. There would doubtless be numerous other women in his life when she was no longer in it, but she was sure none of them would last.

'Let's go,' said Paul. 'The car is waiting.'

They drove along the narrow winding road down the mountain.

'I thought of driving myself,' said Paul, 'then decided against it. I can give my whole attention to you if my chauffeur drives.'

It was a large, open Rolls with a dividing glass panel between them and the chauffeur so that he could not overhear what they were saying. Though even if he could, thought Emma, he wouldn't know what it was about. Very few people in Traj, she had found, knew any English. Krasnovia was a country that had not yet been exploited by tourists. She wondered how long it would remain in this, for her, blissful state. Maybe next time she came there would be coachloads of all nationalities.

It was a wonderful morning of brilliant sunshine and blue skies, but not unbearably hot as it had been when she had arrived the previous day. There, now that they were in the city, were the colourful flower women, the flowers ablaze in the flower beds, the same smiling faces. If the inhabitants of the city had heard the gunfire that morning and been as unnerved as she had been, there was no sign of it. But they were a volatile race. If something sinister were suddenly to happen, their faces would change and their laughter would subside.

They took a road out of Traj into the mountains. The countryside was rugged and magnificent. So very different from England. It was sparsely populated and, Emma thought, a harsh country. Away from the city it was almost sinister.

They reached the top of a mountain and looked down on a vista of rugged rocks with Traj, its villas white in the dazzling sunshine, far below them.

Emma and Paul talked very little. Emma thought that perhaps it was because they had so much to say. Or was it only she who had? And none of it could be said. She felt one moment light-hearted at being with Paul, the next broken-hearted because so soon this idyll would be over.

At last Paul said, 'I hate to say this, but if you are to catch that plane, and I know you must, we should be going back.' He leaned forward and spoke to the chauffeur. And all too soon for Emma they were entering Traj again. Once more there was a procession. The car was forced to slacken speed. Police were stopping the traffic.

As had happened the evening before, so it was again. A crowd of young people with banners, shouting slogans, and a name rose from them : 'Nicky Stagger . . . Nicky Stagger.'

'This is horrible,' murmured Emma.

'It will pass,' said Paul. 'When your husband is out of Traj, it will subside again.'

'I hope you are right.'

'I must be. For the sake of my country. And — '

Paul didn't finish his sentence. Suddenly there was the ear-splitting sound of gunfire. Fierce, short, sharp bursts. A bullet whizzed past Emma, terrifying her. Then another. Paul dragged her down to the floor of the car and shouted to the chauffeur, who shot forward. The procession dispersed to make way.

Emma had never been so frightened. She remembered what Captain Ramon had told her of the attempted assassination — but it had been Paul's wife who had been killed. How easily it could have been her, Emma. How easily this time it could have been Paul.

'That must have frightened you terribly,' said Paul, as a few minutes later they were back in the palace and he helped her out of the car.

'It did, to be honest.'

'To be honest, it frightened me, too. I'm no hero, I assure you, when I am the object of an assassination attempt.'

Now they were on the balcony again and Paul was giving Emma a stiff brandy. She drank it gratefully. She was still shivering from shock, and her teeth were chattering.

'You poor child,' said Paul. 'I feel terribly responsible because I asked you to come here.'

'Please — I'm glad I came. But — well, it was a bit terrifying.'

'Worse than that. If I had dreamed for one moment I was letting you run any risk, I wouldn't have invited you.'

Emma smiled wanly. 'The risk is over for me.' She looked at him anxiously. 'But not for you.'

'I've a charmed life. I must have. I've been in so many tight corners.'

Emma thought if there were ever a man she would trust herself with in a tight corner, it was Paul. As only a short time ago she had proved.

Paul drew his chair nearer to hers and took her hand.

'I said when you came this morning that these were extraordinary circumstances. I say so again. And because of them, can I be absolutely frank with you?'

Her heart trembled. 'Of course.'

'First and foremost, I've fallen in love

with you. It's more than a question of love at first sight, but love at first sound. I fell in love with your voice when I heard it on TV. I'm very susceptible to voices, I cannot bear shrill or harsh ones. But yours — ' He paused. Then he said: 'Do you feel anything for me, Emma?'

'What an unnecessary question!'

'You do?'

'I'm as susceptible to voices as you are.'

His grip on her hand tightened. 'Darling, in view of what has happened, could we perhaps cut the cackle — as I believe they say in your country — and go straight to the point?'

'Yes. Please. Since time is so short, it is what I would like.'

'I'm in love with you, Emma, as I've just told you. You are married, but I believe unhappily so. If you are ever free, I would ask you to marry me. Except — '

'Except — ?'

'You know what happened to my wife?'

'Yes. But we have a saying in England that lightning never strikes twice in the same place.'

'Maybe. But it is not a risk I would want you to take.'

'It is one, once I am free to marry again, I would take willingly.'

He raised her hand to his lips and kissed it. 'Do you realize we have known each other less than twenty-four hours?'

'I do. Does that make any difference?'

'Not to me if it doesn't to you.'

Emma thought of her first meeting with Nicky in Trafalgar Square. Then she had believed she had fallen in love at first sight. So, he had insisted, had he. But how little that had been true of him. Of her, too, she now realized. It had been infatuation, never love. Not love as she was experiencing it now.

Paul glanced at his watch. 'I've said we'll lunch here in twenty minutes. Those minutes are nearly up. But before they are — '

He rose to his feet and drew Emma up from her chair and his arms enfolded her.

'Darling, you may think this crazy, but you must know how much you mean to me.'

'You mean as much to me.'

He held her close and kissed her. Long and lingeringly on the lips. Then, reluctantly, released her.

She sat down again in her chair and he in his. She was aware that the door had opened and lunch was being served.

Paul smiled. 'We timed that rather well, don't you think?'

'Very well indeed.'

'Now we must eat. Are you hungry?'

'Not at all.'

'Neither am I. But as you have a long journey, I insist you eat something.'

Paul said, when they were later having coffee, 'I can phone you at your flat, I hope?' He smiled. 'I have the number.' He looked at her anxiously. 'What sort of a life are you going back to?'

'Not a very happy one.'

'I'm afraid not. And it is all my fault.'

'Of course it isn't. I've been unhappy for a long while.'

'How many years have you been married?'

'Close on two.'

'You were happy at first?' asked Paul, and then said quickly: 'Forgive me, I shouldn't be questioning you in this way.'

'That's all right. You can ask me all the questions you like.'

'And you can ask me any you *like*.'

'How long were you married before — ?'

'Oddly enough, two years. But they were very happy ones.'

'I'm glad. Being unhappily married isn't much fun.'

'It can't be. One day I hope the fates will be kinder to you. And to me.'

'I hope so.'

Paul looked at her searchingly. 'You didn't really answer my question as to what sort of life you were going back to.'

Emma knew exactly what he meant.

And she wasn't such an ingénuée as to pretend she didn't.

'The flat is small. One living-room and one bedroom. I propose to make myself up a bed in the living-room. It will be quite easy. We have a studio couch there on which we have put people up at times.'

'Your husband may object.'

'That will make no difference.'

Paul poured brandy for them both. 'I rarely drink at midday, but today must be an exception. And you certainly need one to fortify you for the flight. Do you like flying?'

'No, though I realize that is foolish. But I'm the coward who dies a thousand deaths. I'm all right once I'm airborne, but I hate take-off and landing.'

'I think most people do. Can I phone you this evening to assure myself you're back safely?'

'Of course.'

'Your husband will be there.'

'He may be. I think in the circumstances he will probably go to his friends. He has a number, though whether 'friends' is the right word for them I wouldn't know. They are all blazing revolutionaries.'

'I'll call you about ten.'

'I'll be waiting.'

'I shall call you every evening. And should there be any emergency you call me.' He wrote a number on a card and gave it to her. 'This will always reach me wherever I am.'

'Thank you. But I hope there won't be an emergency.'

'So do I. I'm trusting you to let me know if your husband acts in any way that may make you think he is returning to Traj. I'm putting him in your care, though I am not sure if that is very fair of me.'

'Of course it is, and I promise you that if Nicky behaves in any way to arouse my suspicions I will let you know at once.'

'We have the code.'

'I won't forget, though I hope you'll never have to use it.'

A manservant came to say that Captain Ramon was awaiting Mrs Stagger. Paul said something to the man that Emma didn't understand.

As he left the room, closing the door behind him, Paul smiled.

'I told him to tell Captain Ramon you will be with him in a few minutes.'

They were both on their feet now. Paul held Emma closely in his arms.

'If only all this were over, darling, if you were free and could become my wife.'

'I shall start divorce proceedings against Nicky at the first moment possible. But until they are through — '

Emma buried her head on his shoulder. She felt very near to tears.

She was silent on the drive to the airport. Captain Ramon, sensing her mood, refrained from his usual cheerful chatter. She wished the next few hours were over; she dreaded seeing Nicky again.

Captain Ramon had a word with one of the officials when they reached the airport.

'Your husband is already on the plane,' he said when he rejoined Emma. He smiled. 'So this is where you and I say goodbye, but I hope you will come and see us again soon.'

'I hope so, too. I've enjoyed my brief stay here. With reservations,' she added.

She wondered if Captain Ramon had any suspicions as to why she had enjoyed her stay so much. What did he know about her interview with Nicky? She found it hard to believe that it was only a brief few hours since she had seen him at the fortress. So much seemed to have happened since then.

Captain Ramon clicked his heels, raised her hand to his lips, bowed, and left her at the steps to the aircraft. A stewardess was there to look after her.

'You seat is in the first-class compartment, Mrs Stagger. Your husband is already there.'

More V.I.P. treatment, thought Emma, and hoped Nicky was appreciating it.

There were very few people on the plane and nobody but Nicky and

Emma in the first-class compartment. She didn't know whether she was glad or sorry about this.

She took a seat across the aisle from him.

'Mrs Stagger, I presume?' said Nicky sardonically. 'I hope you are proud of the havoc you've created.'

Emma sighed. 'Nicky, could we please postpone any post mortems until we reach the flat?'

'Suits me,' said Nicky, and buried himself in a Traj newspaper.

To Emma's relief there were no post mortems when they reached it. Nicky said curtly that he was going out and he didn't know when he would return.

'That's all right with me,' said Emma. 'And, Nicky — ' as he was about to leave the living-room, 'I shall be sleeping in here from now on.'

Nicky shrugged. 'Please yourself.'

He went, slamming the door behind him.

Emma sat down by the telephone and dialled her parents' number.

Her mother answered. 'Emma? Thank God you are safely back in your own country.'

Emma always dreaded her mother in these dramatic moods. Until she had married and left home she had had her fill of them. But she knew she must be tolerant. Her mother had obviously been terribly worried about her.

'How are you and Daddy?' she asked.

'I'm a great deal better now you telephoned. So will your father be. He's out at a parochial meeting, or he would want to speak to you. Will you be in this evening?'

'Yes. I rather want to go to bed early and get a good night's sleep.'

'Daddy will be in around nine and he will telephone you. When can you come down to see us, darling?'

'Where are we? I seem to have lost all count of days.'

'Thursday.'

'I'll come on Sunday.'

'Fine. We're longing to see you.' And after an almost imperceptible pause:

'Will Nicky come with you?'

'I don't think so, Mummy. He has a lot of work to catch up with, so I think his nose is going to be held to the grindstone for quite a while now.'

'Well, we'll look forward to seeing you, darling.'

As Emma replaced the receiver she wondered how much her parents had guessed about her relationship with Nicky. She thought it quite likely that they had realized they had been right when they had begged her not to marry him.

The telephone bell rang again a few minutes later. Emma picked up the receiver expecting the call to be for Nicky. But instead it was Lucy.

'Emma? I've just phoned your mother and she tells me you are home. I can't wait to see you. How about lunch tomorrow?'

'Fine. Usual place, usual time?'

'Okay. I'm longing to know all that's been happening to you. You've certainly hit the headlines.'

'Not willingly,' said Emma. 'But newspapermen will do anything to make a story sound sensational.'

'I like the sound of the President. There was a photograph of him in our paper this morning. He looks marvellous. Tell me, are you alone or is Nicky with you?'

'No, he's out. Listen, Lucy, I've only been back a short time. I'll tell you all the news tomorrow.'

Promptly at ten the telephone bell rang again. This time it was the call Emma had been waiting for.

She gave her number. 'Paul?' she asked, and then swiftly sent up a little prayer hoping that nobody at his end was listening in. 'I'm sorry. I was forgetting. That was a name only to be used when we are alone.'

'We are. At least I am, and nobody would dare to listen in to any call of mine. Anyway, if anyone did, here at the palace, they wouldn't understand it. But how about you?'

'I'm alone. Nicky went out almost as

soon as we returned.'

'I wish you were here, darling.'

'So do I.'

'How are you?'

'A little weary, but otherwise all right.'

'I hated saying goodbye to you.' She heard a sigh at the other end of the wire. 'I wish you were here and I could talk to you. Hold you in my arms.'

'I wish it, too. How have things been in Traj?'

'Quite peaceful. The evening paper said that your husband had returned to England; that was all.'

'No more shooting?'

'No. With your husband out of Traj, I doubt if there will be. He was the firebrand that set light to the torch. I'll call you again tomorrow, around ten. But don't forget that if at any time you want me you've only to telephone me. Good night, my darling.'

'Good night, my love.'

As she replaced the receiver Emma thought what a change there had been in her life during these past few days. If anyone had told her a week ago it would be transformed in this way she wouldn't have believed them. She wondered what the future held in store. She wondered if now Nicky would be content to stay in England, carrying on with his job at the B.B.C., or if he would be simply marking time till he returned to Traj to trigger off yet another revolution. She must keep her eyes open for any danger signs and if she suspected any she must immediately tell the President.

She feigned sleep when some long while later the switching on of the light in the living-room told her that Nicky had returned.

'Emma?'

She didn't answer.

'You asleep?'

She still didn't answer. The light was turned off again and she heard his footsteps going along to their bedroom. A lot of women, she supposed, would have made up the bed for him on the studio couch and slept in the bedroom themselves.

And so she took up her old life again. Except that it was so very different. She had the knowledge that Paul loved her and the realization that she loved Paul, and it kept her sane.

She had lunched with Lucy the day after her return from Traj and said, 'Lucy, if ever you think you fall in love at first sight, think again.' And then a moment later reminded herself that that was what she had done a second time.

She decided to be frank with her parents when she went to see them following her return from Traj.

'You were perfectly right,' she said when they were having sherry before lunch. 'I am not happy with Nicky. Nor is he happy with me.'

Her father looked at her sympathetically. It was only what he had expected. Her mother said sadly, 'Emma darling, I was so afraid it wouldn't work out. What will you do?'

'Divorce him just as soon as I can.'

'Have you evidence?' asked her father.

'Plenty.'

Her mother began to cry. 'My poor little Emma.'

Emma said, more sharply than she intended, 'Mummy, please — I'm not crying, so why should you?'

'I can't bear you to be unhappy.'

'I'm all right. In fact, I think I am happier than I have been for a long while.'

Both her parents looked at her in some surprise. But she wasn't going to enlighten them.

As time passed, Emma sometimes thought she must be living in a dream. She got up, dressed and went to the boutique, lunched with Lucy most days and returned when the day's work was done. Then she cooked dinner for Nicky, who always went out as soon as it was over, and she cleared away, washed up and went to bed.

Madame Eulalie had been delighted by her return. Her little Emma, as she now called her, had brought prestige to her boutique. Customers flocked to be served by her. But only for a while. Before long Emma had ceased to be news.

The only thing she lived for now was Paul's telephone call. Each one became more intimate. Each one brought them nearer together. Nicky was never in. He would return from his work with the B.B.C., sit down to as good a dinner as Emma could cook for him — and she thought some of them were very good indeed — and then off he would go and Emma would wait for the President's call.

So the weeks, the months passed. There came a day when, reckoning it out on her calendar, she found that it was six months since she had been to Traj, six months since she had seen Paul. Her life was routine now. Working each day at the boutique. Meeting Lucy for lunch. Going home on Sundays. She knew that Madame Eulalie would wish it to have been more exciting. It would have brought her more customers.

It was a little before ten one evening when she heard Nicky's key in the lock. She wondered what had brought him home so early. She didn't want him there when she was speaking to Paul.

But it wasn't Nicky who entered the room. Two swarthy-looking men, obviously foreigners, came in, closing the door behind them. She looked at them in astonishment and then in fear. Who were they? Why had they the key to her flat?

'Who are you?' she demanded. 'How dare you come in here like this.'

'We are associates of your husband.'

'What does that mean?'

'You are to come with us.'

Sheer terror held Emma, but she was determined not to show panic. 'I shall do no such thing.'

'You have no alternative.'

Emma's panic deepened. She glanced at the clock on the mantelpiece. It was a few minutes to ten.

'Where is my husband?'

'On his way to Traj.'

Emma's heart thudded. She had been through bad times during her marriage to Nicky, but none equal to this. Then she remembered Paul telling her of the code. When his call came through she only hoped he would realize it was she who was in danger and get help to her quickly.

Even in this moment of danger to herself, she was astonished at this latest development. Nicky had been behaving quite normally lately. They never mentioned Traj. She had been so sure she would know if he had it in his mind to return there. And now he had gone. And it could only be to spark off another revolution. To try to overthrow Paul.

She remembered the two processions in the streets of Traj, the banners with his name held high above the crowd. Remembered Maria, the maid at the hotel, saying that a number of people thought highly of him. Even Paul had admitted he could be a dangerous adversary.

She should have been more on her guard. She had let Paul down.

'We are here on your husband's orders,' said the elder of the men. 'You are to come with us.'

And looking at the two villainous-looking men, Emma knew they meant it. How dared Nicky do this to her? To give these men the key of the flat and send them to kidnap her . . . She had never been so frightened in her life. She glanced swiftly at the clock. It was two minutes past ten. At any moment now Paul would call her. She longed to hear his voice.

'You will come to no harm,' the older man said in a thick guttural voice. 'That is, if you do exactly what we tell you. We know you are close to the President of Krasnovia. He wouldn't wish anything to happen to you. In a few days he will no longer be President and you will be free to return here.'

So that was it, she thought. She was to be kept as a hostage.

'If I suddenly disappear from this flat

there will be a hue and cry,' she pointed out. 'If my parents phone me and find I'm not here they will get on to the police. The people where I work will do the same thing. You can't do this to me.'

'Oh, yes, we can. You will telephone to your parents tomorrow and tell them you are staying with friends in the country for a few days. You will also ring the boutique and tell them the same thing.'

At that moment the telephone bell rang. Emma's heart leaped. This would be Paul's call.

The two men exchanged glances. 'Are you expecting a call?'

'No, but it may be from my mother. I haven't heard from home for a few days.'

'Answer it,' one of the men commanded. 'But be very careful what you say.'

Emma went into the bedroom, followed by the two men, who stood over her as she picked up the receiver.

She gave her number, trying to make

her voice sound normal. But she had an idea that Paul sensed that something was wrong. She held the receiver close to her ear, hoping the men wouldn't hear a man's voice.

'Are you all right, darling?' he asked.

'It's a long time since I've heard from you.'

There was a momentary pause. 'I understand. But it won't be much longer,' he said reassuringly, and her heart jumped as she thought he had most certainly got the message.

'I'm sorry, Daddy, I can't come for the week-end. I'm going to stay with friends in the country for a few days,' she continued, to make doubly sure. She talked of ordinary everyday things for a few moments longer, thinking that if she made the call too short the men might become suspicious. Then she replaced the receiver and made to go back into the sitting-room, but they blocked her way.

'Pack a bag.'

She decided to play for time. 'I've

already told you I don't intend to.'

'And we've already told you we can make you.' The older man took a syringe from his pocket. 'A shot of this won't put you out, but it will make you do as we tell you. You'll be able to walk downstairs all right. We have a car at the door.'

Emma was growing more terrified every minute. If she were in a block of flats it might not be so frightening. If there was a hall porter around. But the flat Nicky and she were living in was over a shop, with workrooms on the first floor. There was nobody else in the building. If she screamed for help nobody would hear her.

'You'd better do as we tell you,' said the man who was obviously the leader of the two.

'Very well. But it will take me a few minutes to collect my things together.'

'We'll stay with you just to make sure you aren't dialling 999,' he said with a tight smile.

Emma pulled her suitcases from

under the bed. She was uncertain as to the best thing to do. Except to take as long as possible before she was ready. Because she was quite sure that Paul in Traj wasn't sitting back doing nothing. He had clearly realized from her use of his code that she was a prisoner, and he would be desperately worried about her. She wondered what was happening in Traj. If Nicky were already there before she could warn Paul it would mean more serious trouble than the last uprising. She didn't doubt that Nicky had planned everything with care. In certain matters he could be meticulous. This plot to kidnap her proved that all too clearly.

'You don't need to take all this time,' the older man told her curtly.

'You can hardly expect me to hurry. My mind's not exactly calm. It isn't as if I'm packing to go away on holiday.'

'We'll give you two minutes longer.'

'Where are you taking me?'

'That's our business. You'll come to no harm if you do as you're told.'

She took a nightdress from a drawer in her dressing-table and then a dressing-gown from a cupboard, and folded them with deliberation. She began to wrap bedroom slippers in tissue paper.'

'Time's up. Close the case. We need to be on our way.'

'I'm in no hurry,' she said as coolly as she could.

The elder man nodded to the younger as he produced the syringe, and they both started to come towards her.

Suddenly there was a noise outside. Her head lifted and the two men paused, the younger one turning swiftly to meet the eyes of his confederate. The next moment the door bell rang.

The man's hand came down heavily on Emma's shoulder. 'Don't answer it.'

She struggled to get free of him, but in vain. The flat was uncannily silent.

The bell rang again, followed by a banging on the door.

'Open up,' ordered a man's voice.

Emma made another desperate effort to free herself, but the hand on her shoulder pressed down harder. She wanted to call out, but didn't dare. Her captor whispered in her ear, 'One word from you and it will be your last.'

She saw that he had in his hand a tyre lever which he held threateningly over her.

She heard the sound of a shoulder being thrown against the flat door. It would open easily with force, she prayed. It was only a very old lock that she had said to Nicky more than once should be changed. How thankful she was that he had been too lazy to do anything about it.

The next moment a police inspector and two constables were in the room.

'Mrs Stagger?' the inspector stated rather than asked.

She was now free of the restraining hand on her shoulder.

'These two men are trying to abduct me. Thank God you've come.'

The inspector nodded to the two

constables, who came forward to either side of the two men.

'You will come with us to the police station,' the inspector told them, where you will be charged.'

'But this is an outrage,' the older man protested. 'She invited him' — nodding to the younger — 'up here.'

'And you came to protect him?' the inspector asked sarcastically.

The two constables marched the men firmly from the room.

Emma collapsed on the bed. She felt terrible. The strain since those two thugs had entered the flat was catching up on her. She knew she must ring the Krasnovian Embassy to warn them that Nicky was on his way to Traj, but she needed a few minutes to collect her thoughts.

'I'm very sorry, but I'm afraid I must ask you to come to the station, too,' said the inspector gently. 'But only for a few minutes while they are being charged.'

Emma nodded wearily. 'But first I

must make a call.'

'Very good. I'll wait for you outside.'

A few minutes later she joined the inspector, who was holding open the door of the waiting police car.

'Your friends are waiting for you at the station,' he told her with a grin. 'They've gone on ahead in the other car.'

She sat back and closed her eyes.

'Did you get your call through all right?' he asked curiously.

'Yes. It was to the Krasnovian Embassy.'

'The plot thickens,' he said. 'It was they who warned the Yard you were being held prisoner. How did they know?'

'It's a long story,' Emma said, 'and I'm too tired to tell you now.'

'Sorry, Mrs Stagger,' the inspector said sympathetically. 'You've had quite an evening.'

8

It was the following day. Emma and Lucy were lunching together. Not at their usual little restaurant where they were regular customers, but in a small one where they had never been before. Emma wanted to be somewhere where she wasn't known.

Lucy was agog to hear all her news. Emma, having told her what had happened the previous night, was now telling her about the scene in the Magistrates' Court.

'Luckily, it was over very quickly and the two men were remanded in custody.'

'You must have been absolutely terrified.'

'I was.'

'Have you heard from Paul since you called him?'

'The phone was ringing when I got

253

back from the police station. It was Paul, terribly anxious about me.'

'Has Nicky shown up in Traj?'

'Not openly, I gather, although he's obviously there. He's probably gone into hiding while he's planning a revolt with his followers.'

'You little thought when you married him that you were going to land yourself in this mess.'

There had been reporters lying in wait for Emma when she left the Magistrates' Court that morning. In answer to their questions she gave the same reply: 'No comment.' It was the same when she reached the boutique. When she left to meet Lucy for lunch, they were still there.

Madame Eulalie had raised her eyes to heaven. 'The good Lord is kind to us,' she said. 'Now we shall have the customers flocking in as we did last time you were in the news.'

The police had assured Emma she had no further need to worry. There would be no repetition of the incident that had happened the previous night. They would see to that. A plain-clothes man would keep watch on the property.

The news of her attempted kidnap was on the radio and television that evening. Guessing it would be, Emma had telephoned her parents. She made light of it, assuring them that they had no need to be concerned about her.

'I don't like the sound of it at all,' her father said. 'And you can guess the state your mother is in.'

'Daddy darling, do try to assure her she's no need to be. Half the trouble is the way the Press blow up a case like this. They're short of news at the moment. Maybe something sensational will happen tomorrow and I'll be forgotten.'

Paul called her at ten o'clock.

'I don't like your staying in London, darling,' he said. 'Not after what happened last night. Couldn't you go away to the country for a few days, somewhere where you are not known?

Tell your Madame Eulalie you need a break.'

But Emma had another idea. 'Why don't I come to Traj?'

'Much as I long to see you, it would be far too dangerous. You must put that idea right out of your head. No, go somewhere quiet in your own country, under your maiden name, where you won't be known.'

'I'll think about it,' she said, not having the slightest intention of doing so. Her mind was made up, but she wasn't going to tell Paul.

'Has Nicky arrived in Traj?'

'Almost certainly. But has gone into hiding. But only temporarily, I'm afraid. He must have been travelling on a false passport.'

The next few days were agony for Emma. She couldn't concentrate on her job. In the end she decided she could stand it no longer. Though Paul had said she must not go to Traj, she was going. She told nobody but Lucy, who she knew she could trust. It so happened that Madame Eulalie was going to Paris for a few days. Emma asked her if she could have a few days off and travel with her, and if she could tell her parents this. Madame Eulalie, to whom intrigue was the breath of life, said she would be only too delighted to have her for a companion. Of course tell her mother and father the truth — that they were going together.

On the flight to Paris, Emma took the older woman still further into her confidence. She was going to Traj, she said, but she didn't want anyone to know.

Madame Eulalie said it sounded like a fairy story.

'And there you will meet your handsome prince and you will marry him and I shall lose one of my most valuable assistants.'

Emma laughed. 'I don't expect it to be as romantic as that,' and thought how wonderful it would be if Madame Eulalie's words could come true.

At Paris she left Madame Eulalie,

whose address she had in case she wanted to travel back with her. From Paris she found she could get a plane direct to Traj.

Her heartbeats quickened as she knew from the different hum of the engines that the plane was losing height. She looked out of her window, and there below her lay Traj. She thought of her first visit and how little she had known what lay before her.

Now that the plane was losing height more rapidly she could see the city mapped out below her. She could see the mountain with Paul's country palace on its summit. What would he say when he found she had ignored his telling her that on no account must she come? Would he be angry with her?

She heard the grating of the wheels as they touched down on the tarmac. There were the usual instructions in various languages that passengers were to remain seated with their safety belts fastened until the plane stopped.

Then they were told they could be

released. The passengers could leave the plane.

The sun was as scorchingly hot as it had been that first day she arrived. As the doors of the plane opened and the steps were put in place for the passengers to descend, a rush of hot air came into the plane.

She picked up her handbag and followed the other passengers from the plane. Everything seemed normal. No sign of tension anywhere. No strain on any of the faces around her.

And then suddenly she saw Captain Ramon. He came towards her with a beaming smile, clicked his heels and kissed her hand.

'How did you know I would be here?'

'I didn't know for certain. But the President thought it just possible. I have orders if you were on the plane to take you straight to the palace. I hope you had a pleasant journey.

'Yes, thank you. I broke my journey in Paris and came on from there.'

'Ah, that explains it. I was here when

the plane direct from London arrived. When you were not on it and I found there was one due in shortly from Paris, I thought I would wait just in case you were on that.'

They drove away from the airport and were soon passing through the city. There were the same women with their baskets of colourful flowers. The same crowded streets. Everything seemed to be going on quite normally.

'How are things out here?' she asked.

'Outwardly everything is normal. But I know the President thinks it is — how do you say it in England? — the lull before the storm.'

'I hope it won't be.'

'So do I, but in a country like Krasnovia one never knows what may happen.'

They were ascending the steep mountain road to the country palace now. There was the President leaning over the balcony as he had been that first time she had seen him.

His greeting of her was warmly

friendly, but no more than that.

'Are you surprised to see me?' she asked.

'Not really. I had an idea you'd come.'

'Even though you told me not to.'

He smiled. 'I'm beginning to know now that you don't always do as you're told.'

'I'll let you know if I want you, Captain,' said the President, and led Emma into the palace.

'I have had a suite prepared for you since the night those men tried to kidnap you, just in case you came,' he said. 'I thought it safer than for you to stay at a hotel.'

A maid appeared and took her cases.

'If you will go with Lucille she will lead you to it, then please come and join me on the balcony.'

The suite was down a long corridor. It might have been a private flat. It had a luxurious living-room and bedroom and bathroom.

'Madame will be comfortable, I

hope,' said Lucille, and Emma was glad to find she spoke English.

'I'm sure I shall be.'

'Would madame like me to unpack her case for her?'

'No, thank you. I'll do it myself.'

Washed and refreshed after her journey, Emma joined Paul. She felt suddenly shy of him. Uneasy as to whether she had done the right thing by coming. But only for a moment. He closed the door as she entered the room and held her in his arms and kissed her.

'It's wonderful to see you, Emma. Even though I am not at all sure you should be here.'

'I've been worrying since I arrived in case you were annoyed at my coming.'

'Darling, no. It is only your safety I'm concerned about.'

'Everything seems peaceful enough here.'

'It could be merely on the surface. That is why I think it wiser for you to stay here at the palace than in the hotel.

Oh, Emma darling, it's so wonderful to have you here.'

'I'd have come sooner if only you would have let me.'

'I'm not going to allow you to stay long. Only a day or two, because I am sure there is going to be real trouble here any day now. I feel it in the air.'

'If there's trouble, I won't want to leave you.'

He smiled and touched her cheek in a little caressing gesture.

'If there's trouble, you will do as I tell you. But let's not talk of that now. Let me just look at you. It's so marvellous to have you here, even if I can only allow it to be a brief visit.'

He held her close again and kissed her. She felt that if trouble were to start that very moment and guns sound, she would still be glad she had come.

Dinner was served on the balcony as it had been on that other occasion when she had been in Traj.

She said : 'It's so lovely to see you again I've lost my appetite.'

'That won't do.' He smiled. 'Actually, I think I have, too.'

When the dinner was cleared away they sat very close together on the balcony drinking their coffee and brandy.

'It has seemed a lifetime since you were here,' said Paul. 'I've thought about you and missed you so much.'

'And I you.'

'It's astonishing how much nearer two people can come even through phone calls.'

'I know. I've thought that often.'

'Was your husband always out when I rang?'

'Always.' Emma gave Paul a brief description of her life since she had last seen him.

'You had no idea he was planning to return to Traj?'

'None at all. The first I knew of it was when those two horrible men suddenly appeared in the flat.'

'That must have frightened you terribly.'

'It did. And I was so afraid when you called me that you might not realize I was using your code the other way round, as it were.'

'I picked that up at once. I rang my Embassy as soon as we finished speaking.'

'Thank God you did.'

'I had a very worrying time till I heard from them that the police had gone to your flat and those two thugs had been taken into custody.'

Emma said, 'I can't think how Nicky could have done that to me.'

Paul leaned forward and took her hands.

'You never really knew that husband of yours very well, did you?'

'I certainly didn't. Do you imagine it will leak out that I am here?'

'I hope not. It's because I don't want it to that I thought it safer for you to stay in the palace.'

'But the officials at the airport saw my passport.'

'I don't think it will matter if it does.

But I'd prefer it not to. Anyway, you are here under my protection.'

'But if there is an uprising?'

'We'll face that when it comes. But I warn you, if anything does start I'm sending you out of the country right away. But don't let's talk about it now. There are so many other things I want to say to you, things I couldn't say when I called you.'

They had left the balcony now and moved into the room. Paul put all the lights out except one shaded table lamp and drew her down on the sofa beside him, his arms encircling her.

'If you only knew how often I've longed to have you here with me,' he said softly. 'How often, too, I had to stop myself from asking you to come.'

'I'd have come, Paul. I longed for you to ask me to.'

He kissed her again, long and lingeringly on the lips.

'It's going to be tantalising having you actually staying here in the palace with me and we can't be together as I want us to be.'

Emma thought of Nicky, of how he had asked her to go back to his flat with him that very first afternoon they had met. How he had assured her that in his country if a man and a woman were in love they went to bed together and didn't let the fact that they weren't married concern them. How different Paul was from Nicky.

'Have you thought about the future over these past few months since we've been apart?' Paul asked.

'Of course I have. I'm going to divorce Nicky. I've already seen a solicitor about it.'

'You have evidence?'

'I know he's been sleeping around.'

'But do you know who with?'

'No. And until I do, my solicitor says I can't go ahead with divorce proceedings.'

'Somehow, I don't think it will be very difficult for you to find the evidence you want.'

'I hope it won't be.'

'And when you're free — then we'll marry.'

'Yes, if that is really what you want.'

'You know it is. I have only one concern, is that what you want?'

Emma's arms tightened round his neck.

'You know it is. I can't believe I have any need to tell you.'

10

The apparent peace of the city was shattered the next day. Paul discovered that a revolutionary news-sheet was being clandestinely circulated announcing Nicky's arrival and that he was setting up secret headquarters. A couple of men circulating the news-sheet were arrested and an unsuccessful attempt was made to kidnap the wife of the Chief of Police to hold as hostage against their release.

Paul told Emma this that evening. She had scarcely seen him all day. He had been so occupied with his advisers and she had kept well in the background.

'This looks like the beginning of trouble,' said Paul. 'The kidnap attempt was foiled, but one wonders what will come next.'

The telephone bell rang and he went

to answer it. He talked for a long while, then replaced the receiver and rejoined Emma. His face was very grave.

'The revolutionaries have taken over a provincial TV station. There's been fighting as my men tried to prevent them, but at the moment it seems they are in control.' He went to his set and switched it on, and after turning the knobs eventually got the station. It seemed to Emma as if there were a lot of people talking at once. She wished she could understand what they were saying.

Then suddenly there was Nicky's face on the screen. She caught her breath, a host of thoughts rushing through her distracted mind. Here was the Nicky who had harangued the rallies in London, who had been cheered by his supporters. Before she had been disillusioned she, too, had been swayed by his oratory.

Now, of course, she had no idea what he was ranting and raving about, but she could guess from the tone of his strident voice that he was full of threats and bombast.

Suddenly the screen went blank and Paul switched off the set.

'I can guess what all that was about,' said Emma.

'I thought you probably would. He was full of threats, insisting that he and the revolutionaries were taking over the country. He — ' He broke off as there was a knock on the door and a servant entered the room and spoke to him.

'I'll have to go,' he said. 'The Chief Commandant of my forces has called to see me urgently. Don't worry, I'll be back as soon as I can.'

Emma waited anxiously. The moments ticked slowly by. She stood on the balcony looking down on the city. Now and again she could hear firing. People's voices echoed up to her. She wondered what was happening and, more fearfully, what was going to happen. She dreaded the thought that Paul would insist on her returning to England, but she was quite sure he would. She supposed it might even be better for him not to have her there. Her safety would only be an additional worry to him.

She wondered if her parents were anxious about her. She hoped not. After all, they believed she was with Madame Eulalie in Paris, and she had only left England the previous day. They wouldn't expect to hear from her for a day or two, and by that time she might be back.

Only she hoped she wouldn't be. She dreaded the thought of having to leave Paul with his country in such a turmoil. His life would be in danger, she was certain. If Nicky's revolutionaries began to succeed — but surely they wouldn't. They were, after all, in the minority. The majority of the country was loyal to Paul.

The minutes seemed like hours. She had never known time pass so slowly. She wanted to go in search of Paul, to beg him to tell her what was happening. But she knew that, of course, she couldn't.

At last she heard his footsteps approaching. He came in and closed the door and she ran into his arms.

'You seem to have been gone such a long while.'

'I know. But there was so much to be settled.' He smoothed her hair back from her forehead and kissed her gently. 'Don't look so anxious. Come and sit down and I'll tell you what's going on.'

'I've been out on the balcony. I heard firing.'

'I know. But only sporadically. That was a nasty business at the TV station. Several innocent men have been killed trying to prevent the revolutionaries from taking over. Martial law is being declared immediately. From now on all cars will be searched. Soldiers will be posted everywhere and patrol the streets.'

Emma shuddered.

'And to think that Nicky started all this.'

'He's had quite a large following for

some while. I told you that last time you were here.'

'I know. But I thought that had all died down.'

'No, it had merely gone underground.'

'How strong are they?'

'It's difficult to say.'

A violent explosion shook the palace. They went out on to the balcony, and down in the city a building was on fire. Emma clung to Paul as a moment later there was yet another explosion. She was trembling all over.

Paul drew her back into the room. He held her closely to him, begging her not to be frightened. They were quite safe up here in the palace.

'But what is going to happen — ?'

Paul said gently, 'I'm going to send you home. Darling, I told you, remember, that if this broke I would insist on your leaving.'

She burst into a storm of tears.

'I won't go, Paul. I won't.'

'You will if I ask you to. If I tell you

that having you here only adds to my anxiety.'

She knew she had no alternative. She had known it all along.

'When do you want me to leave?'

'On tomorrow's plane.'

Tomorrow, thought Emma. This time tomorrow she would be back in England. Miles away from Paul. Not knowing what was happening.

Again a servant appeared and said he was wanted.

'I won't be longer than I can help.'

Another explosion rent the air as he left the room. She went out on to the balcony, standing well back in shadow so that if there was anyone about she wouldn't be seen. More fires were burning. Fire bells were ringing. There were people shouting.

She left the balcony as after a few moments she heard Paul come back into the room.

'I understand your husband has sent a message that if the revolutionaries who are now imprisoned as a result of that TV riot are released, and his party is given power, peace will be restored and he will take over.'

'What message did you send back?'

'None. I decided to ignore his ultimatum. Incidentally, he also said that if I agreed I would be allowed to 'retire' to the country.' Paul laughed shortly. 'My life wouldn't be worth a pigmie if I agreed.'

'A pigmie?'

'The lowest coin we have.'

'How long do you think this will last, Paul?'

'It will be over very shortly, I'm certain. It was only the matter of a few days last time. I believe that by tomorrow things may begin to simmer down.' She knew instinctively that he was only talking so optimistically to reassure her.

'In that case, need I go?' she countered.

'Yes, darling. You are going to leave this poor torn country of mine the very first moment possible. Before anyone realizes you are here. By anyone, I really mean your husband, because if he knew he'd stop at nothing to kidnap you and hold you hostage.'

Emma shuddered.

'Don't you think the news may have already leaked out?'

'I'm certain it hasn't. I can trust my staff here. I know the people who are loyal to me. All the same, I shall be relieved when you are safely on that plane. Captain Ramon will take you to it tomorrow. I only wish I could escort you myself. But that is not possible. I have a meeting with my counsellors in the city.'

'I'll go of course, if I must.'

Paul kissed her.

'That's my very special girl. Remember the first time I called you that?'

'Of course I do. I can remember every single thing you have ever said to me.'

He held her more closely.

'Let's forget our troubles for a little while and I will tell you some more things to remember.'

He told her wonderful things, things such as Nicky at his most eloquent had never told her. He told her he was more deeply in love with her than he had ever believed he could fall in love with any woman.

'And that isn't being disloyal to my wife. We were both very young. Our lives had been easy till the first revolution started. We were neither of us very mature.'

'I'm not sure I'm very mature. All I know is that I love you with all my heart and soul. More than I ever believed it would be possible to love anyone. Oh, Paul — if only I hadn't to leave you. I don't mind the danger. Please couldn't you change your mind and let me stay?' And then quickly, before he could answer her, 'I'm sorry. I didn't mean to ask you that. Forget it.'

'Besides being my special girl you're my brave girl.'

She didn't feel in the least brave, but she wasn't going to tell him so.

At last he said she must go to bed and try to get some sleep. By now it was two in the morning. It had been some time since the last explosion. Paul went out on to the balcony for a moment and returned to tell her that everything seemed quiet. The fires had burnt out. Only occasionally sounds of voices drifted up from the city.

He held her close and kissed her.

'Good night, sweetheart. Try not to worry too much and try to get some sleep.'

'You too.'

He walked to the door of her suite with her and kissed her again. Then reluctantly he released her and without looking back retraced his steps down the corridor to his own apartments.

★　★　★

Next morning, soon after breakfast, Captain Ramon presented himself. As he took her to the car, he handed her a pair of dark glasses to wear.

'In case any enterprising journalist recognizes you,' he said with a smile.

The airport was on the other side of Traj and as she drove through the town she wondered a little sadly how long it would be before she was here again. Certainly everything seemed normal and busy this morning. The traffic flowed spasmodically between the lights and, although it was still quite early, there was quite a large number of pedestrians on the pavements. She was looking idly out of the window when suddenly she became alert. A man, carrying a dispatch case, had Nicky's distinctive springy walk. He was going in the same direction as the car, so she could only see his back, but she believed she recognized the coat he was wearing as the one she had bought for him shortly after they were married. She had to be careful not to draw Captain Ramon's attention to her husband, but a quick glance at the man beside her assured her that he was preoccupied.

Just as the car drew level with the man it was stopped again by the traffic lights. The man paused and turned into a doorway to light a cigarette after putting his dispatch case down against the wall. As the light from the match flared in the gloom of the doorway, Emma realized it *was* Nicky — realized it in spite of the fact that he had grown a beard. But she had seen the tiny mole beneath his left eye which only someone who knew him very well would notice as being characteristic.

At the same moment as Nicky, having lit his cigarette, stepped from the doorway to continue along the street, the lights changed and the car started forward again. For one brief moment, he stared at her. She was even more recognizable than he, for she had involuntarily whipped off the dark glasses to see better. For a moment he stood as though turned to stone. Only his lips moved to curl back in a snarl. When she looked out of the rear window, before the car swept round a corner, she saw that he was once more walking, now very quickly, indeed almost running. *And he no longer carried the dispatch case.* A few minutes later there was a shattering explosion from behind them.

'Another bomb outrage,' Captain Ramon said angrily, 'but we were fortunate. A few minutes earlier and we might well have been caught in the blast.'

Emma suddenly felt sick. Nicky, she realized, had deliberately left the dispatch case in the doorway — the dispatch case which had almost certainly contained the bomb which had caused the outrage and (as she was to learn later) killed a mother and her child of three as well as injuring half a dozen innocent people.

The sound of the bomb had, she realized, blown to pieces the last of any lingering feeling she had for this man she had so misguidedly married. Her only regret was that she had not denounced him to Captain Ramon when she recognized him. But how could she possibly have known that he was bent on murder?

11

Emma put her key in the lock of her flat and felt almost as if she must have been dreaming. There was everything just as she had left it. There were a couple of bills awaiting her and a layer of dust over the furniture. Otherwise she might not have gone to Traj.

She put her suitcase down and flung her coat on the bed. As she did so the telephone bell rang. She hurried to answer it, wondering if it might be Paul.

But it was her mother.

'I just thought I'd take a chance on your being back. You haven't been away long.'

'Long enough to give me a short break. And I'm needed at the boutique. Madame Eulalie doesn't return till Monday.'

'Well, I'm thankful to know you're home. So will your father be. Can you

284

come down on Sunday?'

'I expect so. I'll ring you again tomorrow and confirm it.'

'Do, darling, and come if you can.' A trace of anxiety was now in her mother's voice. 'You're all right, Emma?'

'Of course I am. Only a little tired from travelling.'

'It said on the news this morning there's been a revolution in Krasnovia.'

'So I heard.'

'What a dreadful country it sounds. The sooner you can be free of Nicky the better.'

Before very long, thought Emma, as she replaced the receiver, she would have to tell her parents the whole story. She hoped they would forgive her for not having told them before.

She had hardly replaced the receiver when the telephone bell rang again. This time it was Paul.

'I just wanted to reassure myself that you're back safely.'

'I'm all right, but how are you?'

'Today's been very much the same as

yesterday. There's no sign of any lessening of tension yet. But don't worry, darling. It's bound to take time before things return to normal. Captain Ramon tells me you missed a bomb outrage by minutes. A mother and child were killed and six other people injured.'

Emma was appalled to hear this, and said so. 'Has there been actual fighting in Traj?' she asked anxiously.

'No, the revolutionaries have gone underground.' Paul refrained from telling Emma that the city had been in ferment. Though he knew that the revolutionaries were losing popular support, they still seemed to be very active in guerilla tactics. There was a rumour going about that a foreign power was behind them, backing Nicky and providing arms. If this were true, the trouble could last much longer.

Instead Paul said, 'I'll ring you again around ten this evening. Don't worry if it's a little later. The lines will probably be very busy, and even though my calls get priority there could be a hold up.'

'I hope there won't be tonight.'

She looked round the flat when the call ended. Quickly she dusted it, unpacked her suitcase and put her things away. She looked at her watch. It was barely six o'clock. She didn't feel like staying alone with nobody to talk to for the rest of the evening. She wondered if by any lucky chance Lucy was still at the library.

She rang the number and found Lucy was still there, but was leaving in half an hour. 'How long have you been back?' she asked. 'I'm longing to hear your news.'

'I'm longing to give it to you. Look, couldn't we meet and have something to eat this evening? I'd say come here, but I've nothing in the flat. Besides, I don't feel like staying in.'

Lucy said there was nothing she would like better. As it happened, her uncle and aunt were out that evening, so she only needed to ring and tell the housekeeper she wouldn't be back.

Emma said she would pick up Lucy at the library and they'd find a quiet little restaurant near there.

Later, over their meal, Lucy was listening wide-eyed to Emma's story.

'Strange, isn't it,' Emma said finally, 'that although one was shocked at first reading about bombing and sniping in Ulster, after a time one gets almost used to it. But if you're there yourself, you realize how dreadful it must be all the time for those who have to endure it.'

'Weren't you terrified and glad to get away?' Lucy asked.

'Terrified all right. But I didn't want to come home.'

'Meaning you didn't want to leave your beloved Paul?'

'Meaning exactly that.'

'It's all terribly romantic,' said Lucy.

'The shooting and the bombs weren't. I tried to get him to let me stay, but he insisted on my leaving.'

'Do you think Nicky knew you were there?'

'Perhaps,' Emma said non-committally.

'What was he like on TV?'

'Terrible. Ranting and raving, only of course I couldn't understand a word of it. I could guess what it was all about, though. Anyway, Paul told me.'

'What happens next?'

'I shall go back to Traj as soon as things quieten down. Even if only for a little while. I must see Paul again.'

'I wish you could get someone you could name as co-respondent so that you can divorce Nicky.'

'If he's running true to form, I imagine I should soon be able to.'

Lucy said, 'If things go the way you hope and you marry Paul, it will mean you will live in Krasnovia, I suppose.'

'Of course it will.'

'I hope you'll ask me to stay.'

'You shall be my first visitor.'

Lucy said doubtfully: 'Your parents aren't going to like it very much. Having you so far away, I mean.'

'They won't mind so long as I'm happy. They didn't want me to marry

Nicky, you know.'

'Neither did I.' Lucy smiled. 'Goodness, imagine you the wife of a President!'

'There's quite a lot got to happen before that comes off.'

'Divorce doesn't take as long as it used to,' said Lucy sagely, though she really knew very little about it. 'I saw your mother on Sunday, by the way. I went home for the week-end. She thinks you've been in Paris.'

'I know. I daren't tell her I was going to Traj.'

'Do you know what I should do if I were you?' said Lucy.

'What?'

'Tell your parents the whole story next time you see them.'

Emma frowned. Actually this idea had crossed her mind, but she was by no means sure if it would be wise.

'When are you going home?' asked Lucy.

'On Sunday for the day.'

'Tell them then. It will be far less of a

shock to them when it does happen. You'll probably feel happier, too, once they know.'

Emma wondered if this advice were wise. She certainly wasn't happy at so much going on behind her parents' backs.

'I thought I'd wait till I'd actually divorced Nicky. They know I am going to.'

'And how will you explain nipping off to Traj again once the revolution is over? You can't say you are going over to Paris again with Madame Eulalie. Not if it only lasts a few days.'

'At the moment I don't know how long it will last. But Paul thinks it won't go on for much longer.'

'I take it there's not the slightest chance of the revolutionaries winning?'

This was something that had occurred to Emma, but she had tried to put it out of her mind. She was sure that Paul was confident it wouldn't happen. But supposing he were wrong. If it were true and a foreign power was backing Nicky and providing him with arms, the tide might turn in his favour.

'I'm sure they won't,' she said firmly, and hoped it wasn't only wishful thinking. She glanced at her watch as they were lingering over their coffee.

'I mustn't be much longer. Paul's calling me around ten.'

Lucy smiled.

'Well, your life certainly isn't dull. Don't you sometimes think it's a bit too exciting?'

'No.'

'I wouldn't be as calm as you if I were in your shoes.'

Emma knew she wasn't calm really. She was worrying about Paul every moment.

She heard the telephone bell ringing as she put her key in her door, and hurried to answer it.

'I got through right away,' said Paul. 'I was beginning to think you couldn't be in.'

'I've been having dinner with my girl-friend Lucy. I just felt I couldn't stay alone at the flat. How are things going, darling?'

'The same as yesterday. Sporadic sniping and the occasional bomb shaking the city.'

Again Paul kept from her that the day had been decidedly worse than the previous one. The revolutionaries had blown up the electricity building and there was no light in the city. Buses, too, had stopped running. His great fear had been that the telephone exchange might be the next target, and he wouldn't be able to get through to Emma.

'I wish I was there with you,' she said.

'I'm thankful that you're not. And as you know, I'm not thinking of myself, but of your safety.'

'If you're in danger, I'd prefer to be in danger, too.'

'Sweetheart, we went into this, and you know how anxious I would be.'

'I'm sorry. I shouldn't have said that. It just slipped out. Take care of yourself, won't you?'

'I will. I am the cat with nine lives, as you say in England.'

'You need to be.'

Emma couldn't get to sleep that night, she was so anxious about Paul. She wondered if things really were no worse than they had been the previous day. She had a feeling that even if they were, he wouldn't tell her.

She thought of Lucy's advice that she should tell her parents, and decided it was sound. But it wasn't going to be easy. She dreaded her mother's reactions.

Her mother met her at the station and held her tightly and kissed her.

'It's lovely to see you, Emma. I don't know why, but somehow I wasn't happy about you going off to Paris with Madame Eulalie. I'm not sure I like the sound of her.'

'I can't think why not. She's a pet.'

'She sounds a little crazy from what you've told me about her. Did she come back with you?'

'No, she doesn't return till Monday.'

The congregation were coming out of church as they entered the village.

'I could easily have walked, Mummy; you shouldn't have missed the service.'

'Darling, considering I go twice a day practically every Sunday, I don't think the Almighty will hold it against me if I miss once.'

'Any village news?' asked Emma.

'Esther Whitlock has had twins.'

'She's already got five children, hasn't she?'

'Six. Now she has eight.'

'Is she shattered?'

'Not a bit. She's pleased as punch.'

It was easy to carry on with village talk. When a few minutes after they reached the vicarage the Vicar returned from church, it still continued.

And then later he gave Emma the opening she needed. They were in the drawing-room having coffee after lunch.

'Did you enjoy your jaunt to Paris, Emma?' he asked.

Emma knew she could give him only one answer.

'I didn't stop in Paris, Daddy. I went on to Traj.'

Her mother gave a cry of horror.

'Emma, you can't mean it!'

'I do, Mummy.'

'Then you lied to us when you said you were going to Paris.'

'Only because I didn't want you both worrying about me.'

'And to think your father and I brought you up to be truthful. I'm shocked at you, Emma.'

'Grace, Emma's just said why she didn't tell us the truth,' Robert Lawson said mildly. 'There are occasions in life when a white lie is permissible. Emma obviously decided this was one.'

Emma could have hugged her father. But then, he had always been more reasonable than her mother.

'Why did you go to Traj, darling?' he asked.

'Don't tell me you've patched things up with that dreadful husband of yours,' her mother said angrily before Emma could answer.

'No, Mummy. Of course I haven't. You know I am going to divorce him the first moment possible.'

'Then why did you go to that horrible country?' demanded her mother furiously.

Emma was glad her mother was taking this line. Anything was better than having her dissolve into tears.

She decided she had better make a clean breast of things.

'When my divorce is through I'm going to marry Paul.' She looked from her mother to her father. 'I know you'll both like him.'

'Who is Paul?' asked her father.

'The President of Krasnovia.'

Both parents looked at Emma in amazement. Her father refilled their coffee cups.

'Well, this is certainly news.'

His wife looked completely bewildered.

'Are you serious, Emma?'

'Perfectly.'

'But — but you hardly know him, do you? Oh, I know you met him when you were out in Krasnovia when there was all that trouble over Nicky some months ago, but to be going to marry him — '

'I'm in love with him, Mummy,' said Emma, 'and he's in love with me.'

'But there's a revolution there. It was on the news.'

'I know. That doesn't make any difference.' She gave her parents a brief account of the happenings of the past few days. 'I hoped you'd both be pleased,' she finished. 'I know you want me to be happy.'

'Of course we do,' said her father. 'But it is understandable that we are somewhat taken aback.'

'How old is he?' asked her mother.

'Forty-one. He's a widower.'

'Most unsuitable.'

'Mummy, please don't be difficult over this. It's so vitally important to me.'

'It was vitally important to you when you wanted to marry that dreadful Nicky.'

'I was so young then, so immature. I've grown up a lot since those days.'

'If you had only listened to your father and me,' said Mrs Lawson. 'But then, you always were self-willed.'

'I'm glad I didn't listen to you,' said Emma, 'because if I had I would never have met Paul.'

Her father was beginning to believe that Emma was really seriously in love with her Paul. She had been quite right when she had said that when she had married Nicky she had been so young and immature. She had certainly, as she had just said, grown up a lot since those days. She had an air of self-reliance about her, a purposefulness, as if she knew what she was doing, and was convinced it was the right thing.

Her mother said in bewilderment, 'If you do marry the President, where will you live?'

'In Traj, of course.'

Mrs Lawson burst into tears.

'You, our only child, living so far away in an uncivilized country. I don't know how you can do this to us.'

Again her husband intervened.

'We don't know that Krasnovia is uncivilized.'

'It sounds it. I shan't have a moment's peace with Emma out there.'

Emma said gently, 'Yes, you will, Mummy. You'll be able to come and stay with us often. And imagine it. You'll be staying in a palace.'

This was something Mrs Lawson hadn't considered. She was beginning to feel more and more bewildered every moment. Whereas her husband, also a little bewildered, was beginning to think that Emma could be making an astonishingly good match. Providing the revolution was over and the country settled down once more to a state of peace. In his wildest stretches of imagination he had never imagined his daughter marrying a Head of State.

When Paul called Emma that evening she told him she had been to the country to see her parents and had told them the whole story.

'How did they take it?'

'Mummy was a bit upset at first; but then, I knew she would be. Daddy took it in his stride.'

'I think I am going to like your father.'

'I hope you'll like Mummy, too.' And quickly, because this was what she wanted to know above all else, 'How are things in Traj?'

'Much quieter today.' Paul was thankful to be able to tell Emma this. 'It is indeed now beginning to look as if the revolutionaries are losing ground.'

'Do you think the revolt may be over soon?' she asked eagerly.

'I am hoping so. But one can never be certain.'

'I long to be able to come back to Traj.'

'And I long to have you. But we must both be patient a little longer.'

Emma slept better that night than she had for a long while. If Paul admitted things were better, then they must be. It could only now be a matter of time.

Madame Eulalie, back from Paris the next morning, greeted her effusively and drew her into her little private office, insisting that she wanted to hear all her news.

'Did you have a wonderful time in Traj? Oh yes, I know there was a revolution, but even so — '

'It was all very harrowing,' said Emma.

'Harrowing? What is harrowing? Sometimes there are words in your language even though I 'ave been here so long, that I do not understand.'

'Frightening.'

'Ah, now I know. So my poor little Emma was frightened. That is too bad. And did you not meet your romantic prince? I 'ave been thinking about you a lot while I was in Paris.'

Emma was thankful that an important customer arrived at that moment who insisted on seeing Madame Eulalie herself.

'You must tell me later,' said Madame Eulalie as she hurried out of the office.

Characteristically, Madame Eulalie forgot to question Emma further. The shop was crowded that afternoon and there was scarcely a moment for idle chatter. She had Lucy along to her flat that evening and they had supper together.

'Did you break the news to your parents?' Lucy asked.

'Yes, and all things being considered they took it very well.'

'Don't you feel better now you've told them?'

'Much.'

'There's scarcely a mention of the revolution in Traj in the papers any more. Uncle Tom takes *The Times*, and I always have a squint at it.'

'It can't be now of sufficient importance. After all, it's only a small country.'

'They made enough fuss about it when Nicky was arrested and you went out there.'

'There was probably no news of any importance around at that time.'

There was Paul's usual telephone call

that evening. Lucy left before ten, saying with a smile she was sure Emma would rather have the flat to herself when he was on the line.

'See you for lunch as usual,' she called, 'and thank you for my nice supper.'

Emma lifted the receiver as she heard the front door close behind Lucy.

'Emma?'

'Yes, darling. I hoped it would be you.'

'I've news of Nicky for you. I'm afraid he's been killed.' Paul thought he was wiser to tell her outright. It was hardly a case of breaking it to her gently. All the same, Nicky had been her husband. He hoped she wasn't too shaken. And as for a moment she didn't speak, he said anxiously: 'Are you all right, darling?'

'Yes, Paul. Only — '

'I know it is a shock for you.'

'I just sort of can't take it in. How did it happen? Was he killed in a street battle?'

'He was identified by a police car patrol driving in one of the suburbs, in spite of his beard. They gave chase and in trying to escape he drove recklessly and crashed into a wall.'

Emma could imagine it. Could see Nicky, his face white and distraught, desperately trying to avoid his pursuers. She was surprised that she didn't feel grief. After all, he had been her husband. At one time she had believed herself in love with him. But he had killed that love, as surely as his bomb had killed that mother and child. Now that the first shock was over, Paul might have been talking about a stranger.

'It could be it was better that way,' said Paul gently. 'It was known that Nicky was personally responsible for the deaths of civilians. When peace is restored he would have been tried for murder, and we are not lenient with murderers in this country.'

Emma shuddered. Yes, perhaps it had been for the best that Nicky had been killed in a car crash.

'I think all this will be over in a few days now,' said Paul.

'Thank God, Paul.'

'I say that, too. Most fervently. And when it is — you know what I'm going to ask you?'

'To come to Traj?'

'Yes, and more than that. But we can discuss everything when you are here.'

Emma lived in a daze during the next few days. There were Paul's evening telephone calls, each one reporting that the trouble was subsiding.

She said to Lucy at lunch one day, 'We may not be lunching together much longer.'

Lucy was thrilled.

'When will you be married, Emma? Can I be your bridesmaid?'

Emma laughed. 'I haven't got as far as thinking about anything like that.'

She warned Madame Eulalie that she should think about finding someone to replace her.

'When I go back to Traj, I am afraid I

won't have time to give you proper notice.'

Madame Eulalie beamed.

'I shall miss you, my little Emma, but if it means you are going to be happy . . .'

'I'm sure I will be.'

She telephoned her parents that evening. Rather to her relief, her father answered. She told him the situation.

'I'll call you the moment I know when I'm going, but in the meantime you might prepare Mummy. I don't want her to have a heart attack.'

Her father said he didn't think she had any need to worry on that score.

'Your mother is now quite used to the idea and I think she's thrilled at the thought of having a President for a son-in-law.'

'I'm thrilled at the thought of having him for a husband.'

When Paul called her later that evening he said he had wonderful news for her.

'At last I can ask you to come back here, darling.'

Emma's heart leapt.

'Paul, that's marvellous. Do you mean it's all over?'

'Yes. There are a few pockets of desperate revolutionaries still around, but not a sufficient number to cause any concern. I think Nicky's death has taken the steam out of them, and there was a huge haul of their arms made by the police a couple of days ago. This has caused the foreign power that was aiding them to cut its losses and lose interest. Indeed, they now want to conclude a trade and cultural treaty with us.'

'Oh, Paul, I'm so thankful. I've been praying for this day.'

'Is it too soon to ask you if you can come tomorrow?'

'Of course not. I'll be on the afternoon plane.'

'I'll arrange with our London Embassy to send a car to your flat in plenty of time for you to catch the plane. An equerry will be there, too, with your ticket and to see you off. The plane is running an hour later now and doesn't get in till seven o'clock. I'll book you in at the Palace Hotel as I did the first time you came, and then Captain Ramon, who will meet you, will bring you up here for dinner. I'd meet you myself, but I've an important meeting with my ministers at six that I must attend. But I'll be waiting for you when you get here.'

'I'll be counting the hours.'

'I already have. Twenty-two. Till tomorrow evening, my darling.'

Emma couldn't sleep that night for excitement. It was like a fairy tale. After all, everything was going to come right. She was glad the plane's flight was delayed an hour. It gave her just that little more time to prepare for her journey.

She called at Madame Eulalie's as the shop was opening.

'I've come to say goodbye. I'm leaving for Traj on the afternoon plane.'

Madame Eulalie clasped her to her ample bosom.

'Goodbye, my dear little Emma. I am

so happy for you. I hope everything will turn out the way you want.'

'I'm sure it's going to.'

She had her hair washed and set, and hurriedly bought various oddments she needed. Already she had been preparing for this day. She had a new pale green lightweight dress and coat to travel in, and other new dresses should there be any special occasions.

She had a quick lunch with Lucy, whose eyes nearly popped out of her head when she heard she was leaving that afternoon.

'I'm going to miss you, Emma.'

'And I you.'

'Write to me, won't you?'

'Of course.'

'I wonder where and when you'll be married?'

'That will have to be settled when we meet.'

Lucy gave a little squeal of delight.

'It's terribly thrilling.' And then her expression changed. 'But I'm forgetting — it can't be too soon; you are still

310

married to Nicky.'

Emma was shocked to find how little Nicky's death had affected her. Was she callous that she had scarcely given him a thought since Paul's telephone call the previous night? She hoped not. She didn't mean to be. But it was such a long while now since Nicky had meant anything to her or played any part in her life.

She told Lucy what had happened.

'I don't know what to say,' said Lucy. 'As you know, I hardly knew him.'

For a moment both were silent. Lucy was thinking that Nicky's death now cleared the way for Emma. True, Emma had been going to divorce him, but that would have taken time.

'I've been rather shocked at myself that I've taken it so calmly,' said Emma. 'But I can't be a hypocrite and pretend to a grief I don't feel.'

'Of course you can't.'

They talked of other things till Emma said that time was getting on and she'd have to go.

They kissed each other goodbye.

'Good luck,' said Lucy. 'I'll be thinking of you. Tell your Paul your closest friend says he's a very lucky man.'

'I'm the lucky one,' said Emma, and hurried off back to her flat so as to be ready when the car from the Embassy called to fetch her.

12

As Emma stepped from the plane she saw Captain Ramon waiting to meet her, immaculate as ever in his pale blue uniform. He saluted and kissed her hand.

'It is good that you have come back again. I was delighted when the President told me this morning I was to come and meet you.'

Emma looked around her, smiling.

'It all looks so peaceful, it's hard to believe there has been a revolt.'

As they drove from the airport into the city, there were the flower-women with their colourful baskets of flowers. Everyone looked smiling and happy. The lake reflected the blue of the sky. Emma saw the Fortress of St Mark, where Nicky had been imprisoned, and was glad she only had a brief glance at it as the car passed. She didn't want to be reminded of that dreadful visit to Nicky.

The car drew up outside the hotel she had stayed at on her first visit.

'A suite has been reserved for you,' said Captain Ramon. 'I will wait for you in the lounge while you check in.'

It was almost like her first visit to Traj except that so much had happened since that eventful day. The clerk in the reception desk smiled at her welcomingly. In her suite, Marie was waiting, her smile even more delighted.

'I was so glad, Madame, when I was told this morning that you were coming today and I was to look after you.'

'Thank you, Marie. It's good to be back again. But I'm afraid you have been through bad times since I was here before.'

Marie threw up her hands in horror.

'They were terrible times, but praise be to God they didn't last long. For three days we were without any light, and the buses stopped running, and people were afraid to go out in the streets.'

This was not the picture Paul had given her of the revolt, thought Emma, but she had felt each time he called her that he was keeping from her how bad things really were.

'But now all is peace again,' said Marie cheerfully. 'And long may it last this time.'

Emma went into the bathroom, thinking as she had last time how luxurious it was after the one in her little flat in Fulham. She washed and re-did her face and brushed her hair. Looking at herself in the mirror, she was delighted to find that she was looking her best. Her hair had never looked glossier, her skin clearer and her eyes were shining.

Her excitement mounted as the car drove up the mountain road and neared the palace. It was just as it had been that first time. There was Paul waiting for her. It was the hardest work in the world not to rush into his arms, but she remembered that Captain Ramon was there, and the chauffeur.

But as soon as they were alone, Paul held her close and kissed her.

'If you knew how I've been longing for this moment.'

'I, too.'

He held her from him, looking at her admiringly.

'I'd forgotten how lovely you were.'

She laughed gaily.

'I'd not forgotten how handsome you were.'

'Nonsense. I'm ageing rapidly. I feel it particularly today.'

'You don't look it. And, anyway, why today?'

Paul held her close and kissed her again.

'It happens to be my birthday.'

'Darling, I wish you'd told me. I'd have brought you a present.'

'You've brought yourself. You're all the present I need.'

He drew her down on a sofa beside him, his arms still round her.

'I've said we'll have dinner on the balcony as we did the first time you came.'

They drew apart when a few minutes later the men-servants came to lay the table.

'I'm not a very good host,' said Paul. 'What you must need after that journey is a drink. Would you like the wine we had last time?'

'Please.'

He filled their glasses and raised his to hers.

'Here's to you darling.'

'And to you.'

They clinked glasses and sat out on the balcony watching the daylight fade from the sky and the lights of Traj begin to twinkle in the city below.

'There's so much for us to talk about,' said Paul. 'I don't know where to begin.'

Emma felt this, too. But thank God there was no longer the fear hanging over them that she might have to leave and go back to England.

'Marie, the maid who's looking after me at the hotel, gave me a much more frightening description of the revolt than you did.'

Paul smiled.

'I was as truthful as I dared to be, but I didn't want to alarm you too much.'

'I had an idea you were playing it down. Did your men take many of the revolutionaries prisoner?'

'A surprising number. Indeed, I was shocked to find how many there were. I declared an amnesty when the fighting ceased. Except for those known to be directly responsible for murder of innocent people. I'll tell you, now that it's all over, that it was touch and go for a couple of days last week.'

'That was when I was most worried about you. I had a feeling that I had every reason to be.'

'Tell me more about your parents,' said Paul when they were having dinner.

She gave him a detailed description of her visit to them.

'Will they mind if we're married out here in Traj? I think my people will expect it of me.'

'I've not got as far as thinking about that,' said Emma, and knew she wasn't being entirely truthful. But she knew, too, it must be as he wished.

'They'll come, of course, and any other friends of yours you would like to have here. I'll send the Presidential plane for them. I have two or three friends in London I would like to ask.'

Emma, though she knew her parents would probably like her to have been married at their own little church, knew how thrilled they would be at the thought of the wedding in Traj. She had rather hoped Paul and she could have had a quiet little wedding with only one or two people present, but she supposed as she was marrying the President of Krasnovia this could hardly be possible.

It was after dinner when they had left the balcony and were sitting in his private drawing-room that there was a knock on the door and Captain Ramon appeared. Emma saw instantly from the look on his face that something was wrong. Paul and he spoke rapidly together, and then Captain Ramon hurried from the room.

'Has something happened?' asked Emma anxiously.

Paul hesitated for a moment before replying.

'Yes,' he said bravely. 'The Commissioner of Police has telephoned to say that large crowds are converging on the palace from all directions. There has also been the sound of firing. When the troubles started I gave strict orders that all processions and demonstrations were forbidden, and the Commissioner wished my authority to use force to turn the crowds back.'

'But I thought it was all over, and you'd even granted an amnesty.'

'The Commissioner thinks that is the trouble. They may be attempting a coup now that so many revolutionaries have been released and the country has been lulled into a state of false security.'

'Have you told him to disperse the crowds?'

'No. There are so many it would cause bloodshed. They are my own people. I must at least listen to them. But I have told Captain Ramon if there is serious trouble he is to escort you across the frontier by car. If there is an attempted coup the airport will come under attack.'

'But you? What will you do?' she asked anxiously. And then pleadingly, 'Can't you come away with me to safety, too?'

'Run away?' he asked.

'If there is a coup and you stay, you may be killed.'

'Even so, I must stay. You have courage. You must understand why I cannot run away. Listen . . . '

At first faintly, but with rapidly increasing volume, there was the sound of shouting and tramping feet. It rose to a great din as the people flocked into the courtyard, calling on him to show himself.

'I'm going out on the balcony,' he told her urgently. 'But you stay here, and keep well back from the windows.'

Suddenly there was a brief crackle like the sound of small arms fire and the crowd outside began to chant his name more and more insistently.

Emma clung to him desperately. She knew that on the balcony he would be all too easy a target for a sniper in the crowd.

'No, no, Paul,' she pleaded. 'For my sake, don't go. If you love me, don't go.'

'What is it your English poet says?' he reminded her as he gently disentangled her clinging arms. 'I could not love thee dear so much, loved I not honour more.'

He strode to the window and, throwing back the curtains, stepped on to the balcony.

There was a moment's dead silence which seemed like many minutes to Emma. A searchlight, mounted on a lorry, spotlighted Paul on the balcony. Emma, ignoring Paul's warning, had crept up close to the window but was out of the searchlight's beam.

Suddenly there broke from the crowd a great roar of cheering and Emma realized that the sound like gunfire was caused by nothing more sinister than fireworks. As a set-piece of 'Al Presidenta' blazed in the sky, the crowd began to sing. Paul glanced round and, realizing Emma was so near, held out his hand and drew her out on to the balcony beside him. Her heart lifted. All her fears had now vanished. These people were loyal to Paul. She had no need to be frightened any more.

'What are they singing?' she asked him.

'The Krasnovian version of 'Happy Birthday'.'

There was another burst of cheering as the crowd saw Emma standing beside their President. Paul held up his hand for silence. He spoke to them briefly, happy and smiling, and his words brought even more and louder cheering.

'What did you say to them?' asked Emma.

'I told them that you had done me the honour of saying you will be my wife.'

He waved farewell and the searchlight snapped off. He drew Emma back into the room and pulled the curtains.

'Paul, I'm so glad it was nothing sinister.'

'So am I.' He held her closely in his arms. 'Of course, they disobeyed me by demonstrating,' he added with a smile, 'but then, I suppose every leader must expect to be disobeyed at least once in a lifetime!'

'I am glad they did disobey you,' she said. 'It was a wonderful demonstration of loyalty.'

'Now we can begin to make definite plans.' He kissed her and then raised her chin and looked deep in her eyes.

'Happy?'

'I've never been so happy in my life.'

'Neither have I, my very special girl.'

We do hope that you have enjoyed reading this large print book.

Did you know that all of our titles are available for purchase?

We publish a wide range of high quality large print books including:
Romances, Mysteries, Classics
General Fiction
Non Fiction and Westerns

Special interest titles available in large print are:
The Little Oxford Dictionary
Music Book, Song Book
Hymn Book, Service Book

Also available from us courtesy of Oxford University Press:
Young Readers' Dictionary
(large print edition)
Young Readers' Thesaurus
(large print edition)

For further information or a free brochure, please contact us at:
Ulverscroft Large Print Books Ltd.,
The Green, Bradgate Road, Anstey,
Leicester, LE7 7FU, England.
Tel: (00 44) **0116 236 4325**
Fax: (00 44) **0116 234 0205**

DARK SUSPICION

Susan Udy

When Aunt Jessica asks Caitlin to help run her art gallery while she is in hospital, Caitlin agrees. She hadn't bargained on having to deal with a series of thefts, however — or Jessica's insistence that Caitlin's new employer, Nicholas Millward, must be responsible. Nicholas is as ruthless as he is handsome, but would he really stoop to theft? And what can Caitlin do when she finds herself in the grip of a passion too powerful to resist?

HER SEARCHING HEART

Phyllis Mallet

A proposal of marriage from Robert, whom she does not love, brings Valerie face to face with a frightening question — is she incapable of falling in love? She rejects Robert and flees to the tranquility of Cornwall, hoping to find the answer; but when she meets Bruce and his motherless young daughter Mandy, she discovers new and disturbing emotions deep in her heart — and finds the answer to her question . . .

HEAD OVER HEELS

Cindy Procter-King

Magee Sinclair keeps making costly blunders at her family's advertising agency, so when handsome Justin Kane, head of CycleMania, needs her to pose as his girlfriend for the weekend in exchange for a lucrative campaign, she has little choice but to say yes. Justin needs to cement a deal with Willoughby Bikes by impressing the Willoughbys while they bike trails together. But Magee has landed herself in major trouble — she doesn't know one end of a mountain bike from the other . . .

BACHELOR BID

Sarah Evans

City slicker Benedict Laverton is billed as top prize at the Coolumbarup Bachelors' Ball. To escape the ordeal, he persuades one of the organizers, Rosy Scott, into bidding for him with his own money. But Rosy gets carried away, bidding a cool $10,000 . . . When she goes on stage to claim her man, Rosy not only has to face Benedict's stunned disbelief, she has to kiss him too — a kiss which is spectacular enough to convince her that getting involved with Benedict will end in disaster . . .

SECRET SANTA

Anne Ryan

Jade is a journalist, attached to her boyfriend, Brad, but impossibly drawn to photographer Carl. With Christmas approaching, an exotic Secret Santa gift at work confuses her further, but why does Carl run a mile whenever the heat starts to sizzle between them? Family problems add to Jade's seasonal blues — can she find contentmant before the big day arrives . . . ?